# 10

## *Ten Stories About Smoking*

*by* **Stuart Evers**

**PICADOR**

First published 2011 by Picador
an imprint of Pan Macmillan, a division of Macmillan Publishers Limited
Pan Macmillan, 20 New Wharf Road, London N1 9RR
Basingstoke and Oxford
Associated companies throughout the world
www.panmacmillan.com

ISBN 978-0-330-52515-2

'Some Great project' first appeared, in an early version, in *Litro* magazine.

9 8 7 6 5 4 3 2 1

A CIP catalogue record for this book is available from
the British Library.

Printed in the UK by CPI Mackays, Chatham ME5 8TD

Visit **www.picador.com** to read more about all our books
and to buy them. You will also find features, author interviews and
news of any author events, and you can sign up for e-newsletters
so that you're always first to hear about our new releases.

*For my mother — who once told me
that there is more to a story than
just two people talking.*

# Contents

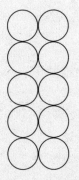

# *Some Great Project*

In the hallway of my grandmother's house sat a glass-fronted bookcase full of hardback novels. Since my grandfather's death they had remained behind the glass, only exposed to the air when she polished the shelves. The books had such fanciful titles, such colourful spines, that I couldn't help myself. The moment she fell asleep, I would steal into the hall, slide open the panes, and thrill at the dusty, bookish smells inside.

When I was about fourteen, I was caught red-handed and cross-legged, two Leslie Charteris novels by my side and *The Killers From Devil Island* open in my lap.

'These are not suitable for you,' my grand-mother said, taking the book from my hands. She held it out in front of her as though it was stinking out the house. 'None of them are suitable; especially this one. Before your grandfather left he told me that I could read any of his books, any one that I wanted, but not that one.'

She leant down and trapped the book behind the glass.

'And did you?' I asked.

'Of course,' she said indignantly. 'And I wish I'd listened to him too. It was absolute filth.'

○

Just before my father died, I informed him of my intention to write a family tree. I expected him, despite his faltering health, to be enthusiastic about the undertaking. But with spittle flecking his lips he told me in no uncertain terms what he thought of genealogy. 'What more do you need to know than I am your father and your mother is your mother?' he said, dressed in his hospital gown, as though to end the matter. On his deathbed he made me reiterate my promise to leave the past be; as did my mother when her turn came.

Once mother's funeral had been arranged, the

service conducted and the legal matters concluded, I fell into a deep, long funk. A blankness overwhelmed me. I didn't think of either of them, alive or dead, but dutifully I tended their graves. Even work, which had long nourished me, did not keep me occupied. I decided then that the only way to escape my lethargy was to embark upon some kind of scheme, some great and meaningful project.

I went to an evening class to learn Japanese, but found that I didn't much enjoy the company of others, nor the unfamiliar character sets. Online chess was mildly diverting for a time but I didn't quite have the patience to truly absorb myself in the game. Long distance running was exhausting but gave me trouble sleeping. Against my better judgement, I went on a few Internet dates and slept with a woman. She cried on my shoulder after it was all over, and promised to call but never did. None of these things were for me.

Then, one afternoon, I did find something: a cache of photographs stacked in the garage. There were boxes and boxes of them; some loose, some in albums, some still in their cardboard sleeves. I took them all into the lounge and over the following weeks catalogued, labelled and scanned them into my computer, ensuring their survival even if someone torched the house or a bomb was dropped upon it. This was steady, uneventful work, but it provided a whole host of other pleasurable tasks. Timelines needed drawing, dates had to be estimated and locations confirmed. The administration was gratifyingly intense, and leafing through those faded pictures of caravanning in Tenby and camping holidays in France brought back memories of happier, fuller days.

After three months I produced twelve uniform, chronologically arranged volumes of photographs. Over the following nights I flicked through each album, adding in my supplementary notes, but I could not shake a returning sense of absence.

When there were no more notes to add, I started looking around for more photographs. One night I became frantic and upended every box and filing cabinet in the house. By four in the morning I was in the loft scratching about with a pen-light, desperate to find something, anything to catalogue. At five, I eventually found something: a heavy suitcase, wedged at the very back of a narrow crawlspace. Inside, packed along with several stale-smelling sheets, I found a pornographic magazine from 1972 and a thick wallet of snapshots.

○

Someone was quite a photographer: the black and white and bleached colour portraits were a far cry from the amateurish holiday snaps in my albums downstairs. They were framed and composed, well balanced; all focused on my father's youthful pout. In the early photographs he is alone, but later he is with a woman, a girl really, in a minidress and sunglasses. They kiss in some of the photos, in others he is stripped to the waist, in one she has her hands over his nipples. The girl looks a little like Jean Shrimpton, but with a slight kink to her mouth.

There were fifty or so photos in the packet. There were pictures of the couple leaning against a Ford Corsair, another one of them on a Vespa, my father without a helmet and with the girl riding pillion. And then some internal shots, portraits of them lying on a brass bedstead covered with rag-rugs and cushions, and then a photograph just of the girl; topless, her hands on her pregnant belly. The next picture was of the girl holding a baby, then the same child in the arms of my father.

○

A secret that my father carried with him for almost four decades took just two days to expose in its entirety. A lifetime's achievement ruined by computers and searchable databases.

○

I gathered as much information as I could, then called a private detective. Two days later the detective showed up at my house and gave me the name Jimmy Tanner as well as the address of a bar in Benidorm. The detective did not look as I expected, he was neither a sharp-suited Sam Spade nor a crumple mac-ed Columbo. He seemed like a regular guy, ordinarily dressed in jeans and a jumper. If there was anything about him, it was the fact that his eyes were hooded. I wondered what he saw in a day, whether the work still excited him.

I looked again at the slip of paper and offered him a cup of tea. He surprised me by saying he'd love one. I warmed the pot and we drank our tea sitting at the round table in the kitchen. I never normally used it and it felt oddly formal, like we were two old ladies discussing the local gossip.

'Was he difficult to find?' I asked, passing him a biscuit. The detective — Andy — took one and shook his head.

'You get used to these things, Mr Moore. Some people make it their business not to be found; your brother wasn't one of those. Army, honourable discharge, then Spain. Simple.'

'He was in the army?'

'Yes, for a good few years too. Personally, I don't know how they stand it. The police was bad enough.'

'You were in the police?'

'Most private detectives are old coppers. They need something to stop them from drinking all day long.' The detective laughed. 'That's a joke by the way.'

I laughed and sipped at my tea. For a brief moment I allowed myself to imagine what it would be like to be the detective's partner, a fellow gumshoe eating donuts on stake-outs and hunting down leads on missing persons. Andy and I would make a great team, I thought.

'Do you miss it?' I asked. 'The police, I mean.'

'I miss a lot of things, Mr Moore, but the police isn't one of them. There's no paperwork now, no desk johnnies telling me what to do, no plastics thinking they know it all. It's just me, an office, a computer and a camera. Some days you're giving folk bad news, but most days it's pretty good news,' he said and smiled. 'Just like today.'

○

I got a package deal and flew out to Spain at the earliest available opportunity. The travel agent tried to point me towards other destinations, places that she said were perhaps more suited to the solo traveller, but demurred when I told her I was visiting family. 'That *is* nice,' she said, 'I just didn't want you being disappointed, you see.'

I was under no illusions. My only experience of Spain was of two business trips, one to Valencia and one to Barcelona; cities whose architectural flourishes, restaurants and culture I fell for instantly. But I had seen enough late night television programmes on the British abroad to know what to expect.

Our transfer took us through the town centre,

all grubby streets and mobs of men, bright signage and lurid advertisement hoardings. It was like an entire suburban British town had got drunk, passed out and woken up on the Spanish coast. When I finally arrived at the apartment complex, the screams from the poolside competed with the constant thud of the beat from a bar over the road. There was no escape, even in my rooms; everywhere I went the air was filled with the heat and howling noise.

On that first afternoon, I opened the door to my apartment, threw my bag on the floor, turned on the air-conditioning unit and slept under its huffing vents. I woke frozen and stiff, my mouth dry and cracked. There was nothing in the tiny fridge and I wasn't sure about the water, so I decided to venture out to the shops.

In the local supermarket I bought water and some wine, a loaf of bread and some instant coffee. The lighting was much too bright, and even behind the lenses of my sunglasses it strained my eyes. The products were mostly familiar, but with odd Spanish brands thrown in, no doubt to appease the locals. The people shopping were all either English or German, and they conducted themselves at a terrifying volume. I paid for my shopping and said *gracias*. The girl behind the counter glared as if to warn me against showing off.

I got back to the apartment and drank a glass of water and a glass of wine on the balcony. I spread out a tourist map over the small plastic table and began working out where my brother's bar, The Throstles' Rest, was located. I looked out over the town, the lights pulsing in neon pinks and greens and slowly began to relax. The screams from the pools were stilled and the breeze whistled against the hem of my trousers. I wondered what my brother was doing at that moment in time, what his bar was like. I hoped we could later share a glass of wine out on the balcony, perhaps even talk about our father.

○

I slept in late and ate breakfast outside, the sun already peelingly hot. I hid myself in the shade and read a novel I'd bought at the airport. It was about a man with a serial killer as a brother; a joke just for my benefit. At 7 p.m. I drank a glass of wine, took a shower, dressed and headed into town.

The main drag of bars, nightclubs and restaurants was fat with people. The air stank of suncream, beefburgers and spilled lager. Amongst the football chants and sportswear, the tan-lines and tattoos, I wandered along, avoiding the pretty girls with their tiny drinks on silver trays. Outside a bar called Susan's I relented and accepted a tequila and shot it down. I felt pink-faced and slightly drunk. Eventually I found the correct turning and zigzagged left then right.

The Throstles' Rest was little more than a shack with plastic windows and a small outside area, but it was just as busy as many of the other places on the strip. And there was no music, save for the soundtrack of a man calling out bingo numbers in a shrill, sad voice.

I poked my head inside and looked around the packed room. It was impossible to tell if my brother was in there or not. A woman with a tray came up to me. 'Sorry, love,' she said in a broad Yorkshire accent. 'Bingo night. Finishes at ten if you fancy coming back.'

O

At a small restaurant I ordered paella and was rewarded with a huge plate that I struggled to finish. I was the only one eating alone and half-way through my meal a duo came on the stage to serenade the diners. A couple – introduced as Mr and Mrs Wright celebrating their sixtieth wedding anniversary – danced slowly as the band played 'Can't Take My Eyes Off You'.

As they danced the waitress came and took my empty plate. 'I gave you an extra portion,' the waitress said. 'You looked like you needed it.' I laughed and paid the bill. It took me an hour to walk off the heavy settling in my stomach.

At ten thirty I arrived back at the Throstles. It was quieter than earlier, though there were still a good few plump men and women sitting around the wooden tables. It was cool inside and sixties music was playing on the stereo. I sat down and the same woman who'd spoken to me earlier put some peanuts down on the table.

'Good to see you back, love. What can I get you?'

I ordered a glass of wine with some ice and looked around to see if there was anyone who looked like an ex-army man. There was only one. He was sitting at the far corner of the bar, a man with a hulking physique that I suspected had once been powerful but had now run to fat. He did not speak to anyone, and didn't look up from his drink. A cigarette burned in his hand. For over an hour I watched him. Just as I was about to leave, he looked up for a moment, almost as if he had just awoken. In the mirror behind the bar his reflection told me all I needed to know.

○

I went to the bar the next day and the day after that. He was always there, but I never quite got a chance to speak to him. Instead I watched closely, trying to get a fuller impression. He seemed never to go to the toilet, never appeared drunk — though he drank steadily throughout the day — and he talked softly when he spoke, which was not often.

On the sixth day of surveillance, I saw my opportunity. The barstool beside him was, for the first time, vacant. I asked him if it was taken and he waved a hand. In front of him were six cigarettes smouldering in a black plastic ashtray. He picked up each cigarette in turn, took a drag, replaced it, and then picked up the next one.

He worked anti-clockwise, then clockwise, anti-clockwise, then clockwise. He smoked those six cigarettes to the filter, then lit six more, arranging them in the ashtray in the same formation.

'Does it upset you?' he said quietly.

'I'm sorry?' I said.

'The smoking,' he said, 'does it bother you?'

'No,' I said, 'no, not at all.'

He grunted and took a quick sip of his beer, then he turned and fixed me with his eyes.

'This one here is Charlie's,' he said, holding up a cigarette and puffing on it. 'This here is Davey's, this one's Butcher's, this one's Damo's and this one's Steve's. And this last one's mine, you see?'

My wine glass was halfway to my mouth, stalled.

'Falklands, yeah?' he said, picking up Davey's cigarette. 'You remember the Falklands?'

'Of course,' I said. He nodded and went back to his drink.

○

The next day the same seat was free. I sat down and this time Jimmy looked up from his cigarette-filled ashtray. He looked so much like my father I wanted to hold him in my arms. But there was a hollowness to the eyes, like there was nothing he hadn't seen and nothing he couldn't do.

'Here again?'

'Yes,' I said. 'I like it here.'

'It's a shit hole,' he said picking up Butcher's cigarette.

'I like the music,' I replied.

He sniffed and tossed a look back to me. He put down Butcher's and picked up Damo's.

'You're the bloke who thinks I'm his brother, aren't you?'

I looked at the glass of wine sweating in front of me. He put down Damo's and picked up Steve's cigarette and sucked on it. I nodded.

'Go home,' he said putting down Steve's and picking up his own cigarette. 'I don't need any more brothers.'

'You have brothers?'

He turned, his face red and urgent.

'Get the fuck out of my pub,' he said.

○

I spent the last day in my holiday apartment listening to the shrieks of children and the admonishments of parents. I sat under the air-conditioning unit, listening intently to every conversation, every sigh, every amplified disagreement. I heard the families leave at night, fathers and mothers sun drunk and their kids running races over the road, car horns blaring at their stupidity. I packed at the last moment, stuffing T-shirts and shorts into my suitcase.

In the cool night air, I thought over and again about what the barmaid – Jimmy's wife – had said when she'd collared me after leaving the bar.

'I'm not one for blame,' she said, 'you make your own rotten luck in this life, I think, but Jimmy? He blames his old man for everything. He says that he only joined up because your bloody father wouldn't go and see him. And as far as he's concerned if he'd not joined up then those boys would still be alive and well. He blames himself, does Jimmy, but he blames your bloody father even more. He replays what happened every day, then has nightmares about it at night. And if that isn't enough, if that isn't hard enough for him to deal with – and me for that matter – you lot keep coming back to remind him all about it.'

'How do you mean, "you lot"?' I said. 'Who's "you lot"?'

She looked at me like I was fooling with her.

'Well you're not the first, are you? I mean, how many more of you are there, anyway?' She turned her back on me and didn't wait for a response.

○

I flew home. A week went by and my sunburn quickly faded. I took some time off work — they said they understood — and spent my days ducking in and out of libraries and record offices. Within a matter of a week I had identified six probable siblings — four brothers and two sisters — and there were several other potential lines of interest.

I gathered all their names, their mothers' names and their family names, and wrote them down in notebooks, then typed up the results on the computer. It was vast, this family tree, there were branches everywhere, twining with other branches and other trees, branches snaking off the page. It was a task bigger and more absorbing than I could ever have imagined.

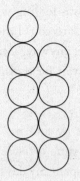

# *Things Seem So Far Away, Here*

Linda liked the way her brother's driveway felt beneath her feet. Shingled and stoned, it gave a solid, satisfying crunch at every step, a sound both aristocratic and forbidden; as though she'd stolen over a wrought-iron fence into the gardens of a stately home. She dropped her cigarette, crushed it under the heel of her boot, and looked at her watch. She was far later than expected, but she didn't think it mattered.

The driveway dog-legged to the right, revealing the white stucco front of The Gables. It was an impressive building. In front of the porch, three snub-nosed cars gleamed as though freshly minted. As she passed them, she wrestled with the urge to kick stones at their fancy paintwork, or smash the wing mirrors with her small ruck-sack.

There was a flash in one of the windows and then Linda saw the heavy front door open. Suddenly, there was Poppy – Daniel and Christina's six-year-old – barrelling towards her, dressed from throat to foot in pale pink fabric. Linda put down her small bag, held open her arms and took the child's running jump full in the midriff.

'Auntie Linda, you're late,' Poppy said.

'And you're ugly,' Linda replied, pulling at her pigtails.

Poppy laughed, and with great effort proceeded to drag a mock-reticent Linda towards the house. Immediately, she started to talk about her ponies and the games they'd play together, and the dress that Daddy had bought her, and the dollies she'd named Patch, Ginger and Princess Lily. As Poppy jabbered, Linda thought it a shame she could not engender such devotion in people her own age.

'Hi there,' Daniel said, leaning against the door jamb. Linda accepted his kiss lightly as Poppy chattered away, pulling on her arm like she was ringing a church bell.

'Leave Auntie Linda alone, Poppy,' Daniel said, rolling his eyes towards his sister. 'Is that all your stuff in there?' He pointed to her rucksack.

'You know me,' she said. 'I always travel light.'

'Can I show Auntie Linda my room, Daddy? Can I, Daddy? Please?' Poppy said, and for a moment Linda was touched; the pleading look on Poppy's face reminiscent of her father's when he was a boy.

'Later, poppet,' he said. 'Let Auntie Linda settle in first.' He flashed a conspiratorial smile towards Linda then bent down to Poppy's level. 'I tell you what, why don't you practise that play you wanted to show Auntie Linda? You know, the one with all your dollies.'

Poppy weighed up the idea, then ran off at pace into the darkness of the house, shouting something unintelligible to either of them.

'She's normally a bit quiet around grown-ups,' Daniel said, 'but she just loves you. When I told her you were coming she started counting down the days. When I tucked her in last night she said: "Just one more sleep and she'll be here!"' He squeezed her arm tenderly, 'You're a hit, sis.'

When he smiled again, his face looked jowly and older. Linda bit her bottom lip.

Daniel picked up Linda's rucksack then rubbed his hands together. It was a familiar motion, something somehow passed along the male line of the family. She could remember Uncle Ron doing the same thing before charring sausages and burgers on the barbecue; also their father before carving the Christmas turkey.

'Christina's just popped out to get some bits for tonight, so why don't we do the tour later and go have a drink in the garden?' he said. 'It's such a lovely afternoon, be a shame to waste it, no?'

'Sounds good to me,' Linda said.

○

Linda couldn't help but feel somehow slighted. Yes she did want a drink, and yes it was a stunning late summer's afternoon, and no she didn't much want to wander around Daniel's lavish house, but all the same, she did want to be given the same deference as the other people she imagined visiting The Gables: lawyers, landscape gardeners, jewellery designers, those kinds of people. Christina, she was sure, would not be out buying 'bits' when they arrived. She would, no doubt, be dressed casually yet elegantly, handing out flutes of chilled champagne and encouraging her guests to help themselves to the canapés on silver salvers.

She swallowed her anger and counted out her breaths. The hallway was dark, with tapestries on the walls and bare lacquered floorboards. It was still and cool, like a museum in a provincial Belgian town, she imagined. This was a house that had a coherent, adult style; there were no posters, no Blu-Tacked concert tickets or Post-it note reminders. Though she was thirty-five – and two years older than both Daniel and Christina – Linda felt immediately gawky and adolescent.

Her Dr Marten boots squelched on the stone flagging of the kitchen – the room longer and wider than her bedsit in Camberwell – then were quiet when they made it out onto a patio area. A long lawn, as fiercely coloured and manicured as any bowling green, stretched out to a well-tended hedge and a five-bar gate, two chestnut ponies snuffling grass behind it. To the right was a swimming pool, inflatable toys bobbing on its surface.

'Please, sit,' Daniel said pointing to one of the cushioned wooden recliners. 'I'll take your bag up and get you a drink. What do you fancy? Tea, coffee, wine, beer, vodka——'

'A beer would be fine, thanks.'

'Which kind? I got some great stuff from a local microbrewery, or——'

'Lager's fine, Daniel,' she said with a smile.

'Right you are,' he said, giving his hands another rub before heading inside.

○

Linda sat and closed her eyes. She could hear birds and the rustle of the trees, and noticed a slightly sour smell coming from her dress that no amount of Impulse was going to mask. She felt, for a moment, that she might fall sound asleep but then a sudden snort from one of the ponies startled her. She opened her eyes and watched them buck at each other, then looked towards the pool. The light breeze blew an inflatable chair across it, a bathing suit draped on one of its arms.

Daniel came back with the drinks and a terra-cotta bowl with a blue glaze. 'For you,' he said. 'Still smoking, I take it?'

'Dirty habit,' she said, taking the cigarettes from the pocket of her jeans.

'We'd prefer it if you didn't in front of Poppy, though. You understand.'

'Sure,' Linda said, a cigarette already in her mouth. She lit it and took a sip of the beer. It tasted good, much better than she thought it would. Daniel wafted the smoke with his hand – another tic that had survived from his teenage years. Linda tipped ash into the terracotta pot and relaxed a little. She was thankful for this concession; she had worried that she'd be forced off the grounds, like at the hospital.

'So,' Daniel said, 'how are you?'

'I'm fine, Daniel. A bit scorched, a bit weary, but doing okay.'

'Rolling with the punches?'

'I don't know any other way,' she said. Linda saw the relief in his eyes: the negotiation of that early, difficult conversation thankfully now over. Her brother then talked at ease about the joys of fatherhood, of the funny things that Poppy said. Linda laughed or smiled at each anecdote, though the humour was predictably lavatorial. Every so often he would remind her of how much Poppy had looked forward to her stay; and Linda would look to the floor, flattered and still disbelieving.

○

She'd only met Poppy on a few occasions, all of them at their mother and father's house in Ashford. Each and every time, the child had refused to leave her side. Perhaps it was the pink streak in her hair, or the holes in her jeans, or the way she sounded so deep and gruff like a man when she sang; whatever it was, it intoxicated Poppy, and confused Linda.

In anticipation of Poppy's birthday, Linda had been knitting her a jumper. Though the September sun was burning that day, it had been a damp and depressing summer, perfect weather for a pullover. Linda had picked out the pattern herself – pink with white horses on the front – and had guessed at its size, hoping it would fit. She was pleased with the way it had turned out.

The process of making it had been hugely pleasurable; each evening, after coming back from the bookshop, she would sit and drink whisky, smoke cigarettes and knit. She got out all her old vinyl and CDs, ones she hadn't listened to for years;

songs that she had loved with devotion, but had, for one reason or another, neglected. Every night, the jumper's slow progress was soundtracked by hard-core and hair metal, dustbowl ballads and country rock, traditional folk and free jazz. One night her neighbour, a pinched divorcee, banged on her door. When she answered, knitting in hand, he asked if he could possibly come in and listen to the Ella Fitzgerald record she was playing. She offered him a beanbag by the chimney breast, and he sat all the way through *Clap Hands, Here Comes Charlie!* After a couple of whiskies he looked red-eyed and far away. As he left he gave her ten pounds for the drinks. She took it without qualm.

'I've brought Poppy a present,' Linda said, cutting across Daniel. 'I know her birthday's not till next week, but . . .'

'Oh, Linda, you didn't need to do that,' he said, the froth from his ale creamy on his top lip. 'Just having you here is enough for Poppy, believe me.'

'Well, if I can't spoil my niece, who can I spoil?' Linda said. She finished her cigarette and mashed the coal into the ashtray.

'Thank you, I'm sure Poppy will love it,' Daniel said and put the beer mug down on the table. He looked pleased; then his smile waned. There was a tentative silence, clicked away by birds and grasshoppers.

'Things seem so far away, here,' she said, 'so very far away.'

'It's certainly relaxing,' Daniel said, 'though the commute is a bitch sometimes.' There was another pause, Linda lit another cigarette; it had been a long journey.

'And you're sure you're okay?' Daniel said. 'It must have been. I don't know . . .'

Behind a cloud of smoke, Linda laughed. She looked at him now, his face stricken with the possibility that she might break down and spill the whole wretched tale. Part of her wanted to; but she spared him, and herself, and instead shook her head.

'I'm okay. Honestly. I have my good days and my bad, but mostly it's all okay.'

'And, of course, there are options, I hear—'

'Daniel,' she said with a sigh. 'When I said things seem far away here, that was a good thing, okay. Can we just leave it at that?'

Daniel nodded and got up to get more drinks. For a moment there was nothing again but the sound of the birds and the grasshoppers, then Poppy reappeared clutching a piece of paper.

'Auntie Linda, look, I've drawn you a picture.'

Linda hooked her fringe behind her ear and invited Poppy onto her lap. It was a child's drawing: out of proportion and garish. Still it was easy to tell who it was supposed to be. For a moment Linda didn't say anything, then remembered herself.

'It's very pretty,' she said.

'It's you,' Poppy said, pointing to the stickish replica. 'You and me.'

'I look sad,' Linda said. Poppy nodded.

'Oh but I'm not sad, Poppy,' she said. 'How can I be sad with you around?' and with that she tickled Poppy who writhed and wriggled and screamed in her auntie's arms.

When Daniel came back with the drinks, Christina was behind him. Linda stopped the tickling and the shrieking subsided. Poppy clambered off her aunt and ran to her mother.

'Look Mummy, Auntie Linda's here!'

'I can see that, Poppy,' Christina said.

O

Linda got up from her chair and accepted a kiss on both cheeks from her sister-in-law. Her perfume smelled expensive, the kind that lingered in the bookstore after rich women had shopped there. Christina wore the scent lightly though, as though she'd almost forgotten she'd applied it. Her hair had been recently cut closely, feathered to show off her delicate features. There was an easiness to the way she carried herself, a quiet yet palpable confidence. She was dressed in dark jeans, ankle boots, and a checked shirt. Though Linda was tall, in Christina's presence this was no advantage.

'Good journey?' she said.

'Yes, fine,' Linda replied. 'Apart from the bus.'

'Oh I am glad. But you must let us pick you up next time, it really is no bother,' she said, putting her hand on Poppy's head. 'Anyway, are you ready for the tour?'

○

Beer in hand, Linda ummed and ahed as Christina – with Poppy as accomplice – explained about boutiques and designers, storage space and bespoke radiators. It was an endless tour of endless hallways with endless doors. Had she been tested on it, as a memory exercise, Linda would not have scored well; there was just too much to take in. Over three floors she saw bedrooms of various sizes, two home offices with views over the garden, several bathrooms and cloakrooms and at least four reception rooms. Yet only two rooms made any kind of impression upon her.

The family room – as Christina described it – was warm and comforting. Linda could imagine them together, the three of them, watching television with their legs tucked underneath their bodies, laughing. There was a lavish fireplace and two big red sofas, so inviting and soft you could sleep there as soundly as in one of the house's many beds. Above the hearth was a triptych of photos that had been printed onto canvas. Linda knew that should anything happen to her brother's family, these were the photos that would be given to the television and the newspapers.

Upstairs, Poppy's room was the perfect kid's retreat. Bright and cheery, it was a practical space, stuffed with toys and educational wall-hangings. Poppy jumped on her bed as Linda nosed around, amazed at the size of the room, at its space. The room she'd had as a child – the one to which she had returned too many times in her adult life – was nothing like this.

'You're such a lucky girl,' Linda said, mussing Poppy's hair. It was an odd thing for her to say. She didn't even believe in luck. Believing in luck, her ex-boyfriend Carl used to say, can only lead to misfortune.

The tour ended at the room where she was to sleep. The floor was covered in a kind of hessian material which gave off a warm, woodsy smell. White walls were decorated with framed line drawings of Wendover and Marlow in the 1850s. The large windows looked out over the swimming pool and there was an en suite bathroom, complete with bath and power shower. It was the cleanest, most comfortable accommodation that she'd ever been offered.

'This is just amazing,' Linda said, 'it's just so gorgeous.'

'It's taken us years to get it right, but we're there, finally!' Christina said.

Christina pointed to Linda's bag, which Daniel had put on a wicker chair.

'Is that everything?' she said.

'I always travel light,' Linda replied.

'Oh I wish I could do the same!' Christina said, suddenly animated. 'My overnight bag looks like I'm moving in for a month,' she said, her unflappable air ruffled for just a moment. Poppy, who had begun to lose interest in the tour, went over to the rucksack and began to unzip it.

'Poppy, leave that alone!' Christina moved quickly to her daughter.

'Why?' Poppy said.

'Because they're Auntie Linda's things and she doesn't want you going through them, that's why.'

'Are there presents in there?'

'There might be,' Linda said, 'but you'll never know if you go on snooping.'

Poppy took her hand from the bag and ran to her auntie.

'I am sorry about her, she can be so difficult sometimes. Anyway, we'll leave you to it. There's plenty of toiletries in the bathroom, you must help yourself to whatever you fancy. The Moulton Brown bath stuff is just heavenly.' Christina put her hands on her daughter's shoulders and pointed her to the door.

'I'll keep this terror out of your way for an

hour or so, then drinks and nibbles for six. Is that okay?'

'Perfect,' Linda said.

○

She took a bath, pouring in a generous amount of honey and almond scented oil. It was so warm the mirrors fogged up and beads of sweat formed at her temples. There was no bath in the bedsit, just a shower that cut out whenever a tap was turned on. Lolling in the water, she felt her body relax; the bedsit, Carl and everything else falling away into the distance.

Using the shower attachment she washed her hair with mint and tea-tree shampoo, then with a jojoba conditioner. The scents confused one another in a pleasing way, rising up thickly from the bath. Out of the water, she went to the shower cubicle and doused herself with freezing water. Her whole body jolted, her jaw clamped shut. She took the cold for some time before turning off the flow.

In the mirror she was partially clothed by the steam, but she could still see where there was the odd scar. Her ribs were plainly visible, her hip bones too; she looked better though, not quite so skeletal, nor so bruised. She thought about a man she'd heard speak at one of the group sessions. He used to put cigarettes out on his own asshole, holding them there until he passed out from the pain. At the time she had not squirmed; but now she flinched at the memory. Scorched but better, she thought. Rolling with the punches.

Dry and dressed in shorts, T-shirt and trainers, Linda took her cigarettes from her jeans pocket, her sunglasses from her bag and bounded down the stairs. Outside, Daniel was filling up the barbecue from a sack with Restaurant Quality Charcoal stencilled on the side. He waved towards her.

'Poppy's having her bath, I told her you'd read her a bedtime story, is that okay?'

Linda nodded and lit a cigarette. The best cigarette of the day. 'No one should ever be too clean,' Carl used to say. 'It's not good for the soul.'

Daniel poured fluid over the coals and struck a match. It took first time. 'Excellent,' he said and came to join his sister. 'Another beer?'

'Can I have a gin and tonic instead?'

'Right you are,' he said and took off his barbecuing gloves to rub his hands before making his way back into the house.

○

The sun was going down, the amber light licking at the water in the swimming pool. From absolutely nowhere, Linda got a violently precise image of living there; of being a functioning part of the family. Picking up Poppy from school, cooking dinner for Christina and Daniel, pouring them a glass of wine when they got home strafed and exhausted. Then leaving them to eat as she got Poppy ready for bed, reading her a story before they kissed her goodnight, stories that would give her a love of books. There would be Enid Blyton and Roald Dahl, *The Wind in the Willows* and *Alice in Wonderland*. And in the summer she and Poppy would swim together in the pool, splashing each other and screaming. She saw them both there, ghostlike and transparent in the water, their faces alight with happiness. Yes. That's the way it would be. She could see it so clearly.

Daniel obscured her view and put down a

highball glass, three ice cubes and a wedge of lime floating in the clear, fizzing tonic. Christina sat down next to her husband, with a glass of white wine. The look she shot at the cigarette was pure poison. Linda ignored it.

'I said she could watch television for half an hour before you read her a story. I do hope that's okay,' she said.

'I love reading stories,' Linda said brightly. 'I help out in the children's department sometimes. They have this story time, and I just love to read out Maisy Mouse and *The Tiger Who Came to Tea* and all those. They love it, the kids, they really do.' She stubbed out her cigarette and realized she sounded like she was in a job interview already. She smiled at them both.

'What books does Poppy like?'

'I'm sure she'll tell you that,' Christina said. 'She changes every day.'

'They do, at that age, don't they though?' Linda said. Christina sipped her wine with obvious enjoyment.

'Yes, I suppose they do.'

O

As the smell of marinaded meat drifted up from the barbecue, Linda lay down on Poppy's bed and read her the opening chapter from *Flat Stanley*. 'My favouritest book in the whole world,' Poppy had said as she placed it into her auntie's hands as though, bomb like, it might explode. It was a title Linda recognized from the bookshop and she read it with the same attention to character and voice that she would at work. Poppy giggled at the funny parts, and was quiet and attentive at all other times.

'I wish you were here every night to read me a story,' Poppy said.

Linda laughed. 'Sure you do, poppet.'

'I do,' she said. 'I wish you were here all the time.'

'Well, I'm here now, aren't I?'

Poppy thought about that as if it were a serious question then looked away.

'Can we ride the ponies tomorrow?'

'Of course,' Linda said, 'we'll do whatever you want.'

'And go swimming?'

'If the weather's nice, sure.'

'And I'll show you my play.'

'That would be great. And if you're very good, I might even give you a present. So time to get on the snuggle bus, okay?'

Poppy put her head down on the pillow, her crooked teeth visible as she smiled. Linda kissed her niece on the cheek and on the forehead.

'Goodnight, princess,' she said before turning off the lamp and walking to the door, wondering where she'd heard the words 'snuggle bus' before.

○

It had become chilly outside, so Christina had fired up the heaters; they smelled strongly of gas and gave off a specific, cloying heat. The table was laden with salads, potatoes, ramekins full of dips and sauces, and a hotplate onto which Daniel was transferring the meat. Christina looked approvingly at her sister-in-law.

'You've been up there ages,' she said, pouring Linda a glass of wine.

'I was *Flat Stanley*-ed into submission,' Linda replied, taking the glass and sitting down. She was starving, the last thing she'd eaten – a cold can of soup – had been lunchtime the day before. She would put on weight here, she realized. She would have to run in the fields, swim in the pool, to burn off the lunches and the hotplates full of meat.

○

Daniel wanted to say that he hoped Linda was hungry but realized this might open onto an avenue of conversation he might later regret. It wasn't so much Linda he worried about, but his wife. Any chance Christina got to probe the emotional hinterlands of her sister-in-law was instinctively leapt upon. It made dinner a precarious business.

Christina's interest always sounded clinical, as though she was studying Linda as part of a greater body of work. At idle moments, perhaps on holiday at their place in Sardinia or when walking out in the woods, she would say to Daniel: 'I wonder what your sister is up to right now . . .' And he would have to endure hours of fevered supposition.

When the two women first met – Poppy had just turned three and Linda was back living with her parents – Christina could barely contain her curiosity. They circled each other: Christina not wishing to scare away her prey; Linda not wanting to appear the unhinged, mad woman in the box room. When they drove home, Poppy full of talk of her new auntie, Christina looked aggrieved, as though she had missed a great and fleeting opportunity.

On their subsequent meetings, Christina had managed to glean more from Linda. But it was never quite enough. Daniel knew this; it was why Christina always invited her to stay, and why Linda had always refused: even in her most fractured state, Linda was a good judge of situation, if not always character.

So why she had accepted this invitation remained something of a mystery. It could, of course, have been that she just wanted to see Poppy for her birthday. Christina wasn't convinced about this, though. She believed that Linda had come because she needed a woman to talk to; as only a woman could understand the full implications of what the doctors had told her. When Christina relayed this theory to Daniel, he sighed and told her she was probably right, even though he knew she was wrong. No one went to Christina for emotional advice. She was too practical, too logical to tackle such complicated issues. To her everything had a solution, an action plan to put into effect. Sometimes his wife reminded him of those old war-time posters he remembered from school: *Make Do and Mend says Mrs Sew and Sew*, *Dig for Victory*, *Loose Lips Sink Ships*; complex problem, easily solved.

Daniel watched the two women talking amiably about Poppy and as they laughed he caught glimpses of the people he had once loved: the sister who would tease him about his acne as she applied make-up in the downstairs toilet before going out to meet her boyfriend at the Locomotive; and the woman who had walked naked across his room the first time they'd spent the night together, paused by the door jamb and said, 'I think I love you already.'

He placed the last steak onto the hotplate and sat down. There were charcoal motes on his jeans and ash in his hair. He told them to tuck in and they started heaping up their plates, the food fresh: potatoes, broccoli, carrots from the garden, the meat sourced from a local farm, the wine brought back from the Sardinian vineyard where their farmhouse was located.

'Isn't the wine good?' he said. 'I think it's the best one we've had.'

'Is it from—'

'Sardinia, yes,' Christina said. 'We went out there at the start of the summer, it's just heavenly. Next time we go, you should come. There's acres of room.'

It was happening; she could feel it. They would ask her, the both of them, perhaps nervously at first but then more sure of their position. They needed a housekeeper, a nanny, a person to go out to Sardinia and open up the house before they went for their week-long break. Someone for Poppy. She would live in that attic room with its hessian flooring and its claw-foot bath and teach Poppy how to play guitar. And Poppy would look at her and say 'I don't ever want you to leave', and she would be able to say, without fear of contradiction, 'I'm not going anywhere, poppet.'

She smiled at her family, her future employers. And though her steak was far too bloody, she ate it anyway, agreeing with Daniel that there really was no substitute for a proper, charcoal-burning barbecue.

○

After they'd finished eating, Daniel took the plates through to the kitchen. The conversation had been gentle; about work, about family and mostly about Poppy. Did he have any other topic of conversation these days? He remembered once talking with conviction on art and music, books and politics, science and religion, but these days he struggled to form a solid opinion on almost anything. Every thought felt sludgy and care-worn, and so he no longer put forward his own views, instead simply reported and rehashed what he read in the newspapers. It was not Poppy's fault, nor Christina's; the blame, if there was any to be apportioned, was all his. Through the French windows he watched his sister smoke nervously. Clearly Christina had begun her exam-ination. Daniel swilled down the last of his wine and went to join them, the word 'barren' repeat-ing in his ears.

'Did you want children?' Christina was saying. 'I mean, not that it matters whether you did or not, I suspect. It's one thing deciding on something, quite another having it decided for you, isn't it?'

Her sister-in-law shrugged and blew out a beam of smoke.

'I've not thought about it much, to be honest, Chris. But when I do, I just think that it's probably all for the best.'

Christina was frustrated that this seemed to end the conversation. She wanted at least a semblance of intimacy. She missed that. At university she'd had four close female friends. They were arts students, drunk and stoned most of the time, crazy and broken and somehow more real than the Chrissie who worked hard and visited the sports hall for circuit training. They liked her, she realized, because she was like a governess or a nanny; always there for practical advice and structure. When they needed emergency contraception, help filling out government forms or applying for loans, it was to her that they turned. In exchange they offered brief insights into their lives.

She had not seen any of them in a decade. The last time, the five of them had met up at the Princess Louise in Holborn. Christina was late, still in the first flush of enthusiasm for her respectably paid job in the city. Arriving into the smoky Victoriana of the pub, she saw them around a small table, talking and laughing, drinking pints of lager and smoking hand-rolled cigarettes. This was, she understood, not a reunion; rather they met up with each other on a regular basis. Her suspicions were confirmed as they talked about shared acquaintances who lived in East End squats. The stories they told were superficial; lightweight tales of money worries and unreliable boyfriends. As she paid for another round of drinks, Christina looked over and thought about how young they all appeared.

Linda was different, she could see it the first time they'd met, a dislocated look in her eyes, a brittleness to her long, starved body. Just being next to Linda made her feel alive and vital, the potential intimacy charging like static between them. Christina looked at her now, across the glass-topped table, her body smoother and less ragged, her complexion clear but her eyes still betraying her confusion. If only she would talk more, open herself up.

'And if you do meet someone you can always try IVF or adopt, can't you? Have you thought about adoption?' Linda put out her cigarette and shot her a wry smile.

'I think I might need a man before I start thinking about the babies, Chris.'

Defeated, Christina drank the last of her wine and suggested a game of Scrabble.

They played Scrabble, then Yahtzee. At just before midnight, Daniel and Christina went to bed, leaving Linda to smoke one final cigarette before going up to her attic room. She was drunk and woozy, not quite yet ready for sleep, but tired all the same. The heaters were off and the air was cooling rapidly. She smoked the last of the cigarette and thought again of the house in Sardinia.

○

She woke early – before six – and could not get back to sleep. Her head throbbed and she drank the whole pint of water she'd put on the bedside table, then went to the bathroom to refill it. There she paused and decided to have a bath rather than go back to bed. She ran the water and poured in the almond and honey oil. The steam made her feel better, her mouth rejuvenated by a vigorous brushing of her teeth. She got into the water and closed her eyes, imagining herself bathing at the house in Sardinia, or soaking herself after a hard day looking after Poppy. Her bedsit seemed so very far away, its dampness, its chill draught and cooking smells. She would not go back: she belonged here, with Poppy.

It felt strange to have a plan, to have a clear and definite strategy, but she liked it. For so long, she felt, she had drifted in and out of life, never knowing what it was there for. But now, in this claw-footed bath inside the huge Buckinghamshire house, it made sense; her childlessness now not quite a blessing but something neat, something explainable. All she needed to do was give Poppy the pink jumper with the white horses on it and show Daniel and Christina just how much the child wanted and needed her auntie. Then the whole plan would fall into place. Daniel would drive her home, she would pack up her belongings and perhaps she'd knock on the door of the pinched divorcee and give him the Ella Fitzgerald record as a parting gift.

Using the shower attachment she again washed her hair with mint and tea-tree shampoo, and conditioned it with the jojoba conditioner. She wrapped it in a towel, turban style, dried herself and then put on the white hooded bathrobe that was hanging on the back of the door. She opened the frosted window and steam wafted out on to the morning air. The swimming pool had leaves bunched at its edges: they would need to be fished out before she and Poppy jumped in later.

Back in her room she went to open her bag and paused. There was a rich and powerful smell coming from the bag, an overwhelming stink of stale cigarettes, and of unaired rooms where smoke had lingered for weeks and months. It caught at the back of her throat; and she thought then of what Carl had said about being too clean. She understood what he'd meant suddenly: only when you're clean do you realize just how dirty life is.

She removed the plastic bag in which she'd put Poppy's jumper. The jumper was wrapped in paper decorated with illustrations of horses. She put her nose to it gingerly, hoping perhaps that somehow the package itself had escaped being tainted with the stench. But it hadn't. It smelled dreadful.

Linda unwrapped it fully just to be sure. The smell was noxious, insufferable, so strong she could feel it taking over the air in the room. She held it towards the light, and noticed that the horses on the front were no longer white but a dirty yellow colour, like old men's teeth. Linda kept it held it up to the light to be sure, but there could be no mistaking the dirt that had embedded in the horses and the jumper.

She saw how the pattern was crooked and the horses difficult to tell from any other kind of animal, that the stitching was erratic and the arms a different length. It looked monstrous. She scrunched the fabric into a ball. As she did there was a loud bang at the door.

'Auntie Linda! Auntie Linda!' Poppy said. 'Are you awake?'

'Don't come in,' Linda shouted, throwing the jumper to the floor. 'Please, Poppy, please don't come in.'

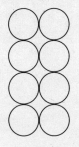

*What's in Swindon?*

The last time I'd seen Angela Fulton she was leaving Wigan's World Famous Winter Wonderland dragging a three-foot stuffed rabbit through a field of dirty fake snow. I'd won the luckless animal for her moments earlier, but it had not proved the conciliatory gesture I'd hoped. Instead, Angela had stormed off in exasperation and hurled the rabbit onto a pile of rubbish sacks by the exit. I watched her leave and in an impotent rage headed to the refreshment tent and got drunk on mulled wine. By the time I got home, all of her possessions were gone.

We were in our early twenties then, the two of us pale and skinny and living in an exacting proximity to each other. We knew no one else in

Wigan, and made no effort to mix with people outside of our respective jobs. Instead we sat in our smoky one-room flat, talking, occasionally fighting and in the evenings making love. Afterwards, by the light of a low wattage bulb, we'd inspect our bodies: the constellations of bruises our bones had made.

How we endured such isolation for so long is hard to say. I suspect now that we found it somehow romantic to live such a shabby, closed-off life. We had no television, no phone; just our books and an inherited Roberts radio that only picked up Radio 4 and John Peel. There was the odd excursion to Liverpool and Manchester, to the Lakes and the Wirral, but for the most part we stayed indoors, paralysed by the intimacy of our affair.

Of course, it could not last, and those last few months were unbearable, horrible. Without either of us noticing it, the real world slowly began to encroach. I started to go out on my own and come back late at night, drunk and insensible. Angela would disappear for hours without ever divulging where she was going. To spite her, one evening I came home with a second-hand television set and

placed it pride of place on the dresser. In retalia-
tion, Angela insulted the way I looked, the length
of my hair, the state of my clothes, the number
of cigarettes that I smoked, my childish sense of
humour. One night she threw a book at my head
and called me a thoughtless fucking cunt. The
next morning neither of us could remember what
I was supposed to have done.

Angela was not my first love, nor I hers; but it
felt like we should have been. Years later, I would
imagine her laughing at the appearance of my
new girlfriend; in idle moments wonder whether
she still dressed the same way. Late at night I'd
remember her naked body, picturing her with a
waxed bikini line that she'd never had. In such
moments, I would consider trying to find her
again, but didn't have a clue where to begin. Still,
the compulsion was there: like a seam of coal,
buried yet waiting to be mined.

○

That morning I left my house and took the
Underground to work, bought a coffee and drank
it at my desk while reading the newspaper. At
9 a.m. there was the usual departmental meeting,

which was swiftly followed by a conference call. I ate my lunch in the courtyard and then browsed in a bookshop. When I arrived back in the office I had nineteen voicemails: three of which were just the sound of a phone being replaced on its cradle.

I answered the emails, returned the phone messages and was about to make my afternoon cup of tea when the phone rang again. It was a number I didn't recognize. I hesitated, then picked up the receiver. There was a pause and then a woman's voice asked for Marty. She was the only one who'd ever called me Marty.

○

Angela sounded exactly as she had before, and I recalled for a moment the way she used to breathe heavily in my ear. She asked me how I was and I stuttered, then stood up for no good reason. There was a pause, a long one. Eventually, I asked her how she'd got my number.

'You're on the Internet,' she said.

'I'm on the Internet?' I said.

'Everyone's on the Internet,' she said.

I asked her what she wanted. She asked if I

was with someone. I said no, not really. She told me she'd booked us a hotel. I asked where. She said Swindon.

'What's in Swindon?' I said.

'I will be.'

'I'm not sure,' I said. 'I mean—'

'Oh come on,' Angela said, 'we both know you're going to say yes, so why waste the time?'

○

I had never been to Swindon before, and all things considered, it is unlikely I will ever go to Swindon again. On the train, there was something about the look on the passengers' faces, a certain kind of blankness. I burrowed into my seat and took out a newspaper, but realized I'd read it all at breakfast. Instead I went to the buffet car and came back with some Chinese nuts and a can of Bass. In the silent carriage, I apologetically opened the can and crunched the snacks. I tried the crossword, but couldn't concentrate on even the simplest clue.

We arrived and in the midst of a stream of impatient commuters, I made my way out of the station. The line for the taxis was long and I

waited behind a couple recently reunited by the
17.04 from Cardiff. The woman had her hand in
the man's back pocket, and he was kissing her.
Even in Swindon, I thought, train station kisses
are the most romantic of all.

Eventually I got a cab, and the driver tried
to engage me in conversation – something about
bus lanes – but I ignored him and looked out
the window, hugging my overnight bag to my
chest. Swindon looked like a business park that
had got out of hand. There was an eerie, almost
American sadness to it; the entertainment parks,
the shopping malls, the parades of smoked glass
office blocks, their windows reflecting the dying
sun. The hotel was at the intersection of several
arterial roads, a squat building cowering against
the flow of traffic.

○

The hotel lobby was shockingly bright, decorated
with plasticky blonde wood. The receptionist – a
young man with ginger stubble – was sullen and
gittish. I told him there was a reservation in the
name of Fulton and he puffed out his cheeks.

'Yes, that's correct, sir. However, the reservation appears to be for a *Ms* Fulton, sir. And we

require the person named on the reservation to be present before any party can take possession of their room or rooms,' he said.

'Did Angela not put my name down as well?'

'Evidently not,' the receptionist said and waving his hand answered the ringing telephone.

I stood there not knowing exactly what to do. 'I'm so sorry,' the receptionist said into the receiver, 'would you mind holding for one moment, madam?' He turned to me.

'Sir, why don't you wait for your friend in the bar?' he said, pointing to some double doors. I picked up my holdall and followed his outstretched arm.

○

The bar was just as plasticky and woody, and just as garishly lit. There was a drunken party of young women sitting around a huge round table and three Japanese businessmen silently drinking Stella Artois. I ordered a gin and tonic. It felt like the right kind of drink to be seen with by an ex-lover – from a distance it could easily be sparkling water. The barman was sullen and gittish. He tried to get me to order some olives. I ordered some olives.

Angela arrived soon after. She looked older, but in a good way. Her hair was kinky and her eyes fizzed like Coca-Cola. She stood at the bar and drank the remainder of my gin and tonic.

'Say nothing,' she said and took me by the hand.

○

The bedroom was brown and cream and functional. She sparkled in her silver dress and pushed me against the wall. For a moment we were twenty again. She guided us both back to a time when we didn't need to worry about interest rates and love handles, pensions and cancer, stunted ambitions and broken dreams. I made sure that she came first; I could have done it with my eyes closed.

○

After we were finished, she looked at me expectantly and rolled over. I held her tightly and she leaned herself back into me. She smelled of sex and shampoo; her breasts heavier in my hands.

'Hello,' she said, 'I've missed you.'

'Me too—'

She interrupted me with a long, sloppy kiss, which she then abruptly curtailed. She put her hands on my chest and then on my face, like she was piecing me together from scrap.

'But . . . no, this is all wrong,' she said. 'Something's not right. I feel . . . ' she shivered. 'I can't explain it.' Angela bent down and kissed me again, experimentally.

'You smell . . . I don't know, wrong,' she said, sniffing my skin.

'What, like bad?'

'No. Just not like you.' She looked puzzled for a moment then glanced at the bedside table.

'Did you quit smoking?' she said, like it was an accusation. I laughed.

'About five years ago now.'

'Quit? I never thought you'd quit. Not ever.'

I didn't like the maddened look in her eyes: she was naked, but not in a good way.

'Well I did.'

I put my hand to her hip and she looked at me as though I had deceived her.

'Do you still drive that Vauxhall Viva?' she said.

'It was a Hillman. And that's long gone. You don't need a car in London.'

She pulled up the bedsheets and put her head in her hands.

'I never should have done this,' she said, 'it was a terrible, terrible idea.' She turned her back on me then and made her way to the en suite bathroom. She had cellulite on her thighs. It was sexy in a way that women just don't understand.

'I don't get it,' I said to the closed door. 'You spent the whole time we were together bitching about how much I smoked and how bad it was for me and how much it stank, and now . . .' She opened the door wearing a white towel. The shower was running.

'Look, Marty,' she said, picking up her abandoned clothes. 'I wasn't going to say anything, but the truth is that I'm getting married.' She smiled, tiredly. 'Or at least I was thinking about getting married. But then out of nowhere, I started thinking about you. About those years we had. And what I have with Declan, well it's not like that. Nothing could be like that. So I had to see. I couldn't let it just go. Couldn't let it just disappear into nothing. I hoped that, you know, that it would all just slot back into place, but . . .'

'But what?'

'Look at us,' she said. 'We're not children any more. In my head, you're this romantic, childish, impossible boy with all these impossible dreams. But that's not you. Not any more. And I can't bring him back. And even if I could, could you really live like that again?'

'Yes,' I said. 'Yes I could. And if that's all it is, I could start again. I could start right now!'

'You know there's more to it than that.'

She laughed and closed the bathroom door. As the water fell I imagined her getting married, the flowers in her hair and the string ensemble playing as she walked down the aisle. Her husband a lunk of a man; his head shaved and looking like a security guard in his hired suit and tails.

When she came back into the room, Angela was fully dressed, her hair wet at the ends. She picked up her overnight bag.

'I'm sorry, Marty, I just needed to know,' she said and kissed me lightly on the cheek.

She shut the door behind her and I went to the window to see her drive away. Across the bypass, a twenty-four-hour supermarket glowed red and blue. I pulled on my jeans and headed out to get supplies.

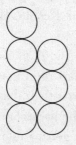

# The Best Place in Town

David Falmer couldn't pinpoint the exact moment he lost control of John's stag party; but he knew it was long before the topic of conversation had turned to hookers. By then it was late, and instead of eating dinner at the Sunbird – a restaurant highly recommended by one of David's guide-books – they were sitting around a smoked-glass table in a neon-lit cocktail bar. Nearby, too close for David's liking, clusters of young Americans stood in short dresses and sportswear, their teeth glowing a ghoulish blue-white. They made David feel old; tired, niggardly and old.

'Little Angels,' John's future brother-in-law, Richard, said. 'You can't come to Vegas and not go to Little Angels. There's like a law against it. It's like the law of the stag.'

Brightly coloured spotlights bounced off the table. David's itinerary was being used as a coaster; Richard had said they didn't need it anyway: he'd been to Vegas loads of times. Whatever you wanted, whether it was the perfect steak and eggs, the finest champagne cocktail, the lowest buy-in Texas hold 'em game or the most enthusiastic whore, Richard always seemed to know the best place in town.

In his broad Yorkshire accent, Richard was describing a Chicana prostitute called Rosalita: her mouth, her legs, her breasts, her behind. David looked to John, hoping to exchange a raised eyebrow; but John was listening intently. Richard was enjoying himself, recreating in lavish detail Rosalita's floor show; the four other men lapping it up. To David it sounded both painful and intensely unerotic. For a moment he wondered whether this was all an act, another of Richard's tall tales, but the details seemed all too plausible.

John leant forward and asked Richard something that was muffled by the sound of a party cheering another stag to down his drink.

'Five hundred in all,' Richard replied. 'And believe me, I'd have paid double that just to see those tits.'

David picked up a spare packet of cigarettes and lit one. He'd not smoked in thirteen years.

○

More drinks arrived and they drank them down, then ordered another round, then another. David watched John laugh, watched the others laugh, and felt like he was watching himself laugh along. He smoked his cigarette down to the filter, the taste uncommon and salty in his mouth. He plucked another from a pack and lit it from the butt of the one he was smoking. He wished he could be sitting outside somewhere smoking that cigarette, anywhere but there, there with Richard and the others. These are my friends, he thought. Phil, Ben, Simon, Dan, John. And I know nothing of them now: nothing. It was as though they'd abandoned their personalities at the airport.

Richard was telling a story about the guy he went to the Little Angels with. He did all the accents and his timing was clockwork; despite himself David laughed along with the others.

He shook his head and tried to hide it, but he was laughing. Richard was a salesman by trade and he'd sold himself to Phil and Ben and Simon and Dan; though David knew something wasn't quite right with John.

On the surface, John seemed to be having a good time, but David could see the clench in his jaw, the same sense of disappointment that had been there the first time he'd got married. This time was supposed to be different: the 3,000 mile journey, the identical suits, the celebration of a man passing from one stage of life to another. But it was not enough. It was not extraordinary; not in the way that John had imagined it. And though John was being loud and boorish, David was sure that part of him was imagining himself there fifteen years before, how it would have felt back then, after Helen, but before Alice, and before everything else.

David missed the punchline of Richard's story and looked out over the room while the men laughed again and reached for their drinks. He saw himself reflected in the glass of the bar and put the cigarette to his lips. His face ghosted behind the smoke, his mouth almost obscured.

'You're smoking?' John said, clapping David on the leg. 'Christ, I haven't seen you smoke in years.'

David shrugged.

'You okay?' John said.

'I'm fine. Just a bit tired. Must be the jet lag,' David said.

'This is my stag, remember,' John said, 'so fuck jet lag, okay? I missed out last time and I'm shagged if I'm missing out this time, so just get a drink down your neck and join the party. I know Richard is . . . I know okay, but he knows all the best places. I mean this is pretty cool, isn't it?'

David nodded, wondering what the Sunbird would have been like, and whether there was any chance of them making the helicopter tour to the Grand Canyon the following day.

'Look,' John said, 'I really appreciate all the organization and stuff, but you've got to be a bit, you know, flexible. What do you think, best man?'

David smiled and crushed out his cigarette.

'I think it's time for a drink,' he said.

The drinks arrived, a pink concoction this time, garnished with a hunk of pineapple. David was about to propose a toast when Richard held his drink aloft.

'To the little angels,' Chris said. 'And the old devils!'

David downed his drink and without a word headed for the toilets.

○

Two hours later, David was quite lost. After leaving the bar, he'd bought some cigarettes and wandered off the strip, turning onto streets without any clear destination in mind. The heat and the cigarettes reminded him of a long sultry summer when he and John had been seeing a pair of Canadian women. Marie, the one David had fallen for, was a tall, tousled-haired girl who liked gin and tonics, painting her toenails and talking dirty. In his single bed they'd lain awake for hours, smoking and watching the sunlight's slow dance on the walls. He could have listened to her talk for ever, and as he walked and smoked, David wondered how and why he hadn't.

John was wild then. His first marriage scared him: one morning of waking and realizing that this was it, there was to be nothing else, had left him petrified. He and Helen were living in an unfamiliar part of town in a rented flat decorated with cast-off furniture from Helen's parents. It was oppressive, all the pieces too grand for a one-bedroom attic flat with a damp kitchen and leaky plumbing. David liked Helen, liked her seriousness and her neat style and clipped intelligence. Her rational, logical nature was balanced by a wicked streak and a breezy sense of humour. She was, as John would later say, far too good for the likes of them.

He walked out on her after six months. He'd been out at some party and had taken the opportunity to get acquainted with one of the waitresses. At two in the morning he hammered on David's door carrying a small rucksack and bag of records. He didn't leave for six years; years that coursed through David as he walked. He smoked and walked and wished that he was with John; younger, leaner, having seen less of the world and of themselves.

He threw down his cigarette and looked around him. For the last few minutes he'd been walking down deserted alleys, those alleys leading on to dusty two-way tracks blown with raggedy bits of paper, flattened cigarette packets and crushed tin cans. He looked around and was faintly relieved to see a shop – Li's 24-hour Liquor store – some way in the distance.

○

A series of bells pealed as he opened the door. It was cool inside and he walked the aisles with a kind of dreamy light-headedness. The store was brightly lit and the rows of products, comfortingly recognizable but different, Americanized, looked almost fake under the fluorescent lamps. He touched the handle on the refrigerator door, held it, then opened it. He took out a bottle of root beer and then made his way over to a display case that held three donuts: his body clock was confused enough to believe that this was breakfast and those items the closest he could find to such a meal.

The man behind the counter looked up from a black and white portable television. He rang up the items and said something which sounded like five dollar twenty. David fumbled with his wallet and handed Li – if that's who he was – a ten. The change was placed on the counter and the man went back to his television programme. David stood there for a moment, unsure what to do. He had planned to ask for a taxi number, eat his makeshift breakfast and then get back to the hotel, change out of his suit, go down to the pool and swim, then shower and go to sleep in the huge bed with the silky pillows. But for a moment that all seemed a preposterous idea. He picked up his coins, his bag of donuts and the root beer and left the shop, the door jingling like loose change as he exited.

Outside it was fully dark, the sky pricked with stars and spilled light from far-off casinos. David sat down at a concrete picnic table and tucked in to his donuts. They were slightly stale, the glaze dry and powdery, and he ate them quickly without any real enjoyment. He cracked the seal on the root beer and took a long pull on it, the medicinal smell reminding him of the times he and John used to hang around in the Newbury branch of McDonald's, drinking root beer through plastic straws and talking about Susan Tucker, the sixth former who worked the Saturday shift.

He lit a cigarette and looked up and down the road. There were no cars or people, no lights even. He kicked a stone with his boot and spat for no other reason than there was no one to see him do it. Just as he did, the man from the shop came out, took a pack of Camels from his pocket and lit one.

'Delphinium?' he said.

'I'm sorry?'

The man gestured with his cigarette behind him.

'You go Delphinium? Everyone come here, they all going. I can tell, you going Delphinium.'

David didn't know how to respond, but smiled a big dumb smile and hoped that would do. But the man from the shop then sidled up to David and tugged at his jacket sleeves. He had his cigarette wedged into the corner of his mouth.

'Look — Delphinium,' he said, pointing to a cluster of lights in the distance. 'Good casino, best in town.'

The man looked around, his face confused and wrinkled. 'Where's car?'

'I'm sorry?' David said.

'You no come in car?'

'Oh, I see. No. I walked.'

The man tugged on his sleeve once more and pointed to a thin fenced-in track. 'Ten minutes. Fifteen most. I use for motorbike.'

At the end of the pathway were the lights, and they were enticing. He squinted his eyes and the colours went to pixels. The man urged him forward and David started to walk rather slowly along it. He wondered then whether this was entering into a trap. Whether he would be later bludgeoned or murdered, or robbed then raped. But he couldn't go back, couldn't now ask for the taxi number or a ride back to the strip. It was the Delphinium or nothing. The man was waving him on, and David was smiling, feeling trapped even out in the open expanse of the desert.

'Tell them Li sent you,' the man said almost as an afterthought. David waved back, determined he would do no such thing. When he got to the Delphinium he would have a drink, a cocktail of some kind, and then get the concierge to call him a taxi. He thought about that as he walked, the cocktail – a whiskey sour he was thinking, or maybe a Martini – and the taxi, or perhaps a limo. Yes, he thought, a limousine; imagine the looks from the stag party as he tooted the horn, their blank faces as they wondered whether he'd won a million on the slots. Yes, he thought, cocktails and limousines, home and bed.

○

It took twenty minutes to arrive at the fifties-style facade of the Delphinium Casino and Hotel. It was brightly lit by two large searchlights and was swarming with people. Uniformed valets whisked away broad-finned cars as doormen greeted their owners at the revolving doors. The people entering the casino were different from the kind he'd seen at the tables and slots on the strip. They were smart, these people; couples mainly: the men in sharply fitted suits, the women in elegant, flowing gowns. At the door, the bouncers said hello to every well-dressed patron.

David straightened his tie and ran his hands through his thinning hair. One drink, he told himself, and then he'd call a taxi. He could hear the chatter, could feel the excitement of the patrons flooding through the door.

'Good evening, sir,' the doorman said. 'Welcome to the Delphinium.'

○

Inside, the lobby smelled richly of tobacco, leather and freshly cut flowers. Men and women streamed through it and down the grand stairway. At its foot, the dark smoky bar area was full; groups were talking and drinking, some sat at booths, others around round tables; others standing, cigarettes aloft in long holders. Once through the door, David paused, taking in the sound of women's heels on marble, of muffled conversations, of soft piped music. 'Isn't this just to die for?' a woman wearing an emerald dress with silver brocade said to her companion as she walked by. 'Isn't it just divine?'

Realizing he was blocking the door, David walked slowly in the couple's wake, passing two payphone booths and the reception desk, thinking of just how much John would have loved this place: its clubby gentility, its well-dressed women and effortless American chic. Ava Gardner would fit in here, he thought, Frank Sinatra, Dorothy Parker, but most of all John. He could imagine him, drink in hand, talking his way around the room like he'd been born to do just that, a smile on his lips and women swooning at his accent.

David reached the stairs and was about to descend to the bustling bar when a man hailed him. He was slick-haired and wet-lipped, his face that of utmost concern.

'Excuse me, sir, can I perhaps be of assistance?'

David looked at the man, then at the staircase. 'I'd just like to have a drink, actually, if that's okay.'

The man smiled and looked slightly relieved. 'But of course, sir,' he said. 'You may also like to know that Miss Amelia will be on stage in' – he took out his pocket watch and looked at its face – 'a little under fifteen minutes. She will be performing in the Oak Bar, which is through the double doors to the left of the bar area.' With that he bowed his head, clicked his heels and walked off towards reception.

David moved slowly, slightly confusedly. He heard snippets of conversation, the high giggling laughs of flirting women, the gruff chuckles of men. He could not keep his eyes from the tables. If the men looked like movie stars, the women – their hairstyles curled and coiled, their waistlines obviously cinched by corsetry – seemed otherworldly. Their make-up was immaculate, and when David's glance fell on one of the women for too long, his was met with a look of withering contempt. Embarrassed, he kept his head down until he reached the bar.

'Hello, sir, what can I get you?' the bartender

said. Like the earlier employee of the hotel, he was impeccably dressed with an oiled widow's peak and a manicured pencil moustache.

'I thought a cocktail,' David said. 'It seems everyone else is drinking cocktails.'

'A wise decision, sir. And is there a particular cocktail you would like . . . ?'

'Well, I did think—'

'Begging your pardon, sir, but I would recommend the Manhattan. I pride myself on making the finest Manhattan in the county.'

David lit a cigarette and nodded. 'A Manhattan sounds great, thank you.'

O

In the nearest booth, three couples were discussing their Malibu beach homes, the problems of domestic staff and plans for a Parisian holiday. One of the men had recently bought a Triumph Thunderbird motorcycle and was talking about it in rapturous terms. The woman to his right said that, as far as she was concerned, it was absurd to be scared about the big things in the world when you could die at any moment – especially on the back of a motorcycle.

'Oh, Bunny, what a mind you have!' her companion said. 'Do you really see the same tragedy in a motorcycle accident as you do in global apocalypse?' He was biting down on a thin cigar and wore rimless spectacles. His gas-blue suit was snug on his shoulders.

'Oh you do tease me so, Harry. You know perfectly well what I mean. How you die is immaterial. Whether alone or with the whole of the world: the effect is all very much the same,' Bunny said. Her hair was braided, her dress a thin slip of black velvet.

'This,' an overweight yet not unattractive man said wagging his finger, 'sounds dangerously close to politics. And we all know the rules where that's concerned.'

'It's more . . .' Bunny said, drawing on her cigarette, 'a philosophical issue, wouldn't you say so, Harry?'

'I wouldn't know; I care little or nothing for either,' Harry said. 'What I *can* say is that no matter how much of a death trap it is, no matter if it could cause a thermonuclear war, I wouldn't give up that Thunderbird. Not ever.'

His wife, a bird-like woman with blonde bangs

and a small scar on her chin, put her gloved hand on his jacket sleeve.

'And I'm glad too. He's such a dreamboat with that thing between his legs.'

They laughed, all of them, and David looked away hurriedly in case they caught him eavesdropping. He crushed out his cigarette and hunted in his pocket for the fold-up map of the strip and its environs. Part of him felt vindicated for leaving the party; the other deeply disappointed that he hadn't come across this place either online or in one of the many guidebooks he'd bought. He opened out the map and took a sip of his cocktail. Then another more lengthy one. It was divine.

'Is the drink to your satisfaction?' the bartender said.

'Yes,' David said. 'It is . . . delicious.'

'Can I perhaps get you another, sir?'

'That would be wonderful, thanks.'

But the bartender stopped his effortless drift to the bourbon and bitters and glanced down at the counter.

'Excuse me, sir,' he said with a bowed head. 'But could you possibly refrain from reading at the bar? It is, I'm afraid, against the hotel rules.'

'Oh,' David said, 'I'm sorry, I was just trying to —'

'I understand of course, sir,' the bartender said, deftly folding the map and handing it to David, 'but this is a bar in which people should feel comfortable. And our patrons tend not to feel comfortable with clientele who arrive alone and sit at the bar reading. I do hope you understand.'

David looked around the room and down at the space where his map had been. He put the folded-up map inside his coat pocket. The bartender placed a silver bowl filled with cashew nuts in front of him.

'Thank you, sir,' the bartender said. 'I'm glad you understand.'

○

By the second Manhattan, David wondered if he was drunk or simply hallucinating from the heat and the walking. To his right an amorous couple sat in a small two-person booth. They were talking in low voices with a restrained, almost prudish vocabulary. Still it seemed to be doing the trick for them; the man's hand was on her thigh and pressing for higher. His partner – a woman who was not his wife – was only pretending to stop him. David felt hot under his suit and he undid the top button on his shirt. He tapped his hand against his packet of cigarettes and wondered where the others were. In a limousine, more than likely, in a car taking them to the edge of the city.

The couple stopped their petting and stood, as did the three couples in the larger booth. David looked over his shoulder at them. They were like dolls, animated things swishing through large double doors.

'If you wish to catch Miss Amelia, sir,' the bartender said, 'it might be wise to make a move to the Oak Room. A waitress will serve you at your table.'

'What kind of songs does she sing?' David said. 'I wasn't. I mean, I didn't come here specifically to see her, so . . .'

'She's wonderful,' he said. 'She plays a mean version of "Summertime". And "As Time Goes By" and "Moon River". She has a voice like smoke on velvet.' He smiled wistfully and went to attend to another customer. He was a square-jawed, quarterback type and he leaned over to the bartender, slipping him a bill. The bartender looked at his fingernails and another bill was produced. Then the man rejoined his group, placing his hand at the base of his wife's spine.

David looked around at the room. There was barely a soul in there now, just a few couples too wrapped up in each other to care about the music. And there was no music. No background music at all. There was the rush from the other room, the smattering of applause, the sound of low talk, but nothing else. No trills of mobile phones, no slot machine jingles, no noise bleed from headphones, the air was untroubled: as relaxed as an old, soft shoe.

'I need to go and run an errand. Can I make you another drink before I go,' the bartender said.

'Er, no I think. I think I should be getting back to the hotel now.'

'Are you not staying with us, sir?'

'No. I'm staying at the—'

'I'm sure sir doesn't need to tell me all of his business, now, does he? So can I get you one last drink for the road?'

David looked at his watch but he didn't now know whether it was six in the morning, six in the evening or six o'clock British time.

'Okay, yes I will. But can I ask you a question?'

David said. 'Why is it that you're not in any of the guidebooks, or on any of the maps?'

'Oh that's quite simple, sir,' the bartender said, 'the management believes that marketing is crass and unnecessary and only attracts the kind of clientele unsuited to the Delphinium.'

He put the drink down on a paper napkin. 'Enjoy, sir,' he said. 'I will be right back.'

○

When the bartender returned it was with the quarterback. An old Bakelite phone was passed from behind the bar and the man had a low urgent conversation with someone.

'You'd think he was having an affair, wouldn't you?' a voice said. David turned round to see a wild-haired man, greying at the temples, a thin beard and dark glasses. He was wearing a silver lamé lounge suit with a southern bow tie. The bartender made his excuses to David and hurriedly put a beer down next to the man.

'But the thing is you never can tell, can you? You just never can tell.' And with that he started to laugh; laugh like he couldn't stop. He put his hands up as if to apologize and hailed the bartender.

'Hey, bud, get this guy a drink. My shout.'

The bartender went back to his bourbon and the man next to David offered his hand to shake, his mouth withholding his amusement.

'Name's Flagstaff.' David drank the last from his glass and looked at the man. He had friendly, hound-dog features and a drinker's nose. He shook his hand.

'David. David Falmer.'

'Well, David Falmer, you're a long way from home, ain't ya?'

'I came here by mistake,' David said. 'I was out walking, and then, you know, suddenly I was just here.'

'Sometimes that's the best way to find what you're looking for, man,' Flagstaff said and went back to his drink. He started to laugh again and managed to choke on his beer trying to hide it. Beer suds matted his beard and dripped onto his suit. He wiped away the foam and laughed out loud.

'Oh man, you should see your face! What a picture. What a fucking photograph! I've been watching you for a time now and I still can't believe it. Tell me this, I mean really, tell me you don't really think that this is all for *real*, do you?'

David thought of the perfect hairstyles, the cigarette cases, the vintage watches.

'I'm sorry, I don't—'

'Horseshit, buddy boy! You thought' – Flagstaff was rocking back and forth on his barstool now – 'shit, what did you think? That this was some kind of Las Vegas Brigadoon? That all these people were ghosts or some shit like that? Christ, you English are dumb. I've met a lot of English people and they've all been dumb, but you? You're the dumbest I ever met.'

He slapped the bar hard. David felt the contagious nature of the laughter.

'I never really . . .' David said, suddenly realizing how stupid he'd been. 'So what the—'

'What the fuck is going on? Good question, pal, good fucking question.' He sucked on his bottle of beer and moved his stool closer to David.

'Through there is some woman singing songs written before these people's grandpappies were born. She's Cold War Chic, Miss Amelia, and all these are her Cold War Kids. That's what they call themselves, Cold War Kids. It's all just make believe. Just a bunch of phoney fucking rich kids dressing up in their grandfathers' suits and their grandmammy's petticoats. They run around pretending like it's nineteen-fifty-two, or maybe it's nineteen-fifty-five, I can never remember. Last week they had a pretend three-minute warning and all of them spent the night in the fallout centre in the basement. Happy fucking days, right?'

Flagstaff drained his beer and beckoned the bartender over. 'Check this out,' he said with a smile.

'Say, bud, can you get me another beer and maybe some of those cheese crackers you do?' The bartender nodded. 'Oh and can you confirm the exact year it is? I'm going a bit senile, you know?'

'For the last time, Mr Flagstaff,' the bartender said, 'such talk is strictly against casino policy.'

'You see!' Flagstaff said. 'What a bunch of fucking phonies.'

Flagstaff laughed and despite himself David joined him. He saw himself sitting there, slack-jawed, and realized how stupid he must have seemed. They clinked glasses and Flagstaff bought another drink. They fell into an easy conversation about why young men and women would want to relive years that they hadn't experienced.

It was the kind of discussion he would have once had with John: light, funny, but with just enough seriousness to keep it from frivolity. They were the conversations which would end with John telling a truth, a long rambling truth about his life. The fact of his mother's death, his workaholic father, his easy infatuations and the guilt he still felt about Helen. The abortion, the dreams that had been crushed under the weight of his own expectation and his own laziness.

David would listen and offer no advice save for a comforting nod, or the occasional 'I see'. But that John, the John who talked with a soft candour, late at night, had long since been boxed up and packaged away. There were no doubts now, no uncomfortable barking dogs in the back of his mind, just dates and times and plans and resolutions. And when he thought about it like that, David realized how wrong he'd got it all.

'I should get going,' David said. 'I've left my friend and . . . I just need to get back.'

'Gee, Dave, I'm hurt. I thought you were sticking around for my act.'

'I'd love to but . . . I really need to get back.'

'Gimme a cigarette,' Flagstaff said. 'I'll give you a sneak preview before you go.'

Flagstaff took a Zippo lighter from his pocket and lit the cigarette. He inhaled once then blew out a perfect circle, then a perfect square, then an equilateral triangle. David was stunned, a memory coming back fully formed.

'Oh my god, you're the smoking guy!' David said. Flagstaff looked up at him and smiled the widest, maddest smile David had ever seen. Flagstaff kept smiling and blowing squares and circles and triangles.

'Must be twenty-five years ago, now,' David said, 'but I remember it so clearly. Remember *you* so clearly. You had long hair then and this big old beard and you blew all these shapes. Impossible shapes. It was the best thing I ever saw on *Paul Daniels' Magic Show*, I mean honestly.'

Flagstaff's smile faltered, then disappeared. His eyes went dark and narrow. It felt like the whole room had gone silent.

'Don't you ever mention that cocksucker's name around me, okay? Ever.'

He blew out a Star of David.

'Daniels . . . Daniels is a fucking louse. A bald fucking dwarf with a rug that wouldn't fool a drunk Ray Charles.'

He knocked back his drink and blew a pentagon. David must have looked alarmed, so Flagstaff put a hand on his arm.

'Look, Dave, I'm sorry. I didn't mean to be so . . . I don't know, but it still cuts me right to the quick. Twenty-five years later and still it cuts me. See, I was supposed to open for Daniels on his world tour. Back in eighty-three. Two hundred dates worldwide, television specials, you fucking name it. He gives me the contract and I push him for more of a cut of the door. The management, they give me a little extra but not as much as I wanted. I tell them that I'm a draw, that I'm selling 'em out every night. My manager tells me to take the deal, that I've pushed them as far as they'll go, and I say I'll think about it. That weekend I go out and get high. Get so high I don't remember nothing about it, so high no one finds me for a week. My manager's all trying to hush it up and he's pretty certain that Daniels' people haven't found out. We do a rehearsal show and I fucking rock the joint. And that's when Daniels sees how much the audience loves me. The putz got scared. I mean he was real scared, jealous as all hell.'

He blew a perfect hexagon and laughed.

'Or at least that's what I thought at the time, right? I'm not naive, even back then my act was, shall we say, not without its controversy? But fuck it, the deal was on the table and I should have taken it. Should have bitten Daniels' fucking hand off, but ha ha, I knew best. Guts of the young, right? Only a fucking idiot would have pushed it. Everyone was telling me to sign on the line that is dotted, but I was too busy playing a pissing contest with a midget magician. By the time I'd calmed down, Daniels had already won and had offered the slot to some fucking trapeze artist or something.'

He shook his head and blew a complicated series of shapes that eventually formed the American flag.

'Thing is that a few months before, back when we were still friendly, Daniels had warned me about throwing things away. We were backstage in the bar, after the show you saw. We'd had a few drinks and I was asking him how a such a short, ugly dude like him had managed to get a prime-time television show, a sexy blonde and a two-hundred-date world tour. He turns to me and says: "You know what, Flagstaff, I don't know. All I do know is that you only get one talent in this life. Whether it's god-given or comes from your genes or your DNA, I don't know either. But Flagstaff. I do know that you only get one talent. Only one. So you best make the most of it while you can."'

The smoke faded and he blew on the end of his cigarette. He chuckled to himself.

'Not much of a philosopher, that Daniels, but he was right. Maybe if I'd listened I'd have signed that deal and racked up enough money for my retirement and then I wouldn't be here telling fifty-year-old jokes, blowing smoke ring elephants and jacking off in my dressing room. Listening's always been a problem for me. I hear, but I don't listen.'

Flagstaff rolled his cigarette in the ashtray, then put it out. David thought of John, the old flat, his Canadian girlfriend and all the times he had listened, every time he'd given a well-placed hand on the arm, or offered the softness of 'I understand'. David said, 'I'm good at listening, actually. It's what I do best, I suppose.'

To this Flagstaff just laughed, patted David on the back and said so long. By his drink a pale smoke trunk and a pair of tusks hung in the empty air.

○

An hour or two later, David opened the door to his hotel room. John was curled up in an easy chair, rocking slightly. He was in his underwear, his hair ruffled and an empty bottle at his feet. He didn't seem to notice David come in.

'I'm sorry,' David said. 'I lost track of time. I went for a walk see, and before I knew it I was out in the middle of nowhere, I mean, really lost . . .'

David wanted to tell John all about Flagstaff, about the casino, and its clientele, but the words died on his lips. He could see that his friend was shaking, his body stuttering in the twilight.

'Are you okay?' David said. 'What the hell happened?'

John looked at his friend and then to the floor. 'I don't want to talk about it,' John said. 'I don't ever want to talk about it.'

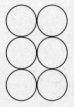

# *Underground*

For several years he had spun a solid and convincing story about an inherited sleeping disorder. It had been passed down, he claimed, on his mother's side of the family and it meant he often woke up screaming, or was unable to sleep at all. It wasn't anything to worry about, he'd reassured her with his arms hooked over her ribs, it was just a part of him, like his height or his shoe size. 'Doctors call them the night terrors,' he'd said with a wry smile. 'Makes them sound like some old aristocratic family, doesn't it?' She'd laughed a little and then kissed him. He slept right through that first night, and slept for many nights afterwards.

Some weeks later, when the attacks first began, Jean felt prepared for them. She woke instinctively and immediately tried to calm him. She held him tightly and felt the erratic beat of his heart; she stroked his hair and told him that he was safe, that she'd got him. Peter lay in her arms immobile. When she tried to hold his hand it did not easily yield and when it did, it did so grudgingly. She spoke softly, reassuringly, saying the very first things that came into her head. She talked about her dreams and her ideas for the house they would own; the cars they would drive, the places they would visit. And she held him close until he eventually drifted off to sleep. This went on for months. By the time they moved into their three-bedroomed house, however, she had become accustomed to his screams and shudders, and neither now woke her in the night.

Her father and mother had been a pair of sometime insomniacs. As a teenager, she was used to getting up in the night and seeing one or other of them sitting on the sofa, perhaps reading a magazine or sipping a hot drink. Sometimes she would stay up with them; other times just get a glass of water and take it back to bed. She always thought this was normal, so she was surprised to discover that her first husband could sleep through just about anything. She'd always found this somehow creepy. 'I was dead to the world,' he'd say and she'd think what a perfectly horrible phrase: so chill and unpleasant. That the marriage lasted less than a decade was not solely down to his sleeping, though she couldn't help but believe it betrayed a fatal flaw somewhere deep in his character.

Peter's flaws were more obvious, apparent from the moment she first met him. It was the company summer party and he had been coerced into attending by his boss. Jean had never seen him before – he was a consultant – and he looked uncomfortable. He was dressed in a slovenly suit, with persistent flakes of dandruff on his shoulders, pricks of sweat on his top lip. They were in a garden under attack from an abundance of greenfly. An unfortunate woman in yellow was covered in them, dots of them sticking to the fabric of her dress. Jean was standing next to him when they both saw the woman – Kathy from sales validation – lose her patience and try to brush all the insects from her skirt.

'I bet you're glad you didn't wear yellow,' Jean said to him.

'Quite,' he said. 'It would clash terribly with these shoes.' He smiled, quickly. Jean was quietly disarmed.

She introduced herself and they talked about work. Jean made spiteful comments about her colleagues, pointing out their indiscretions and unpleasant habits. He laughed and sipped at his wine, commenting where it seemed appropriate. When there was no one left to dissect, Jean suggested that they leave the party, discreetly and separately, and reconvene in the car park. She went first and Peter finished his wine, wondering whether she would still be there in five minutes' time.

The car park was deserted and she stood by a wooden fence, talking on her telephone. Her summer dress exposed her legs, her wedge espadrilles making her look taller, a lazy gust of wind fingering her hair. As he walked towards her Peter buttoned up his jacket, then unbuttoned it. When she noticed him she ended her call and told him she knew of a restaurant nearby: it wouldn't take long to walk. She linked her arm with his and they chatted about how strange it was that they had not met before.

They ate outside a Spanish place, picking at fish and meats in tiny terracotta bowls. Jean did most of the talking, and he listened intently, his head leant on his fist, his maroon tie loosened and splayed. Around them it got dark; couples left and arrived. They drank a lot of wine and told their own little stories. He spoke with a slight drawl to his accent that might have been Irish or Scottish. She liked it whichever country it was. When the bill arrived, they split it and he did not suggest a nightcap, nor did she invite him to her flat for a coffee. Instead they kissed as it started to rain, two cabs arriving within minutes of each other. They had each other's numbers and that itching feeling that something had imperceptibly changed.

O

Over the weeks, she bought Peter medicated shampoo and took him shopping. He went along without argument, enjoying the attention. She took him to her favourite salon where her stylist gave him a haircut he initially eyed with suspicion, but later came to like. It wasn't quite a transformation, more a remodelling. Every day he thanked her, even though sometimes she was unsure what she was supposed to have done.

Jean read up about night terrors, but didn't discuss her research with Peter. Whenever sleep was mentioned, she felt him stiffen and so she let it go. At his flat, a high-ceilinged place in Edgbaston, she would select CDs at random from his collection and listen to them while he cooked. She had heard of almost none of the artists and she was surprised at how fragile and brittle the singers and recordings sounded − like people trapped on another planet. She liked that he had passions and enthusiasms she did not share, the faded, slightly bohemian feel to the place, the framed prints that hung on every wall.

It didn't matter whether they stayed at her place or his, the night terrors kept him awake most nights − despite her early attempts to wear him out with vigorous lovemaking. After an attack he would remove himself from the bed and go to the bathroom. There he would wash his face, brush his teeth, shave, then head into the lounge and watch television. He'd pour himself a drink or two and return later to the cooling bed, his body fresh with the smell of cosmetics and the alcohol.

They went on several holidays together, and were introduced to each other's parents. The meetings were stiff and formal, though Jean's father and Peter bonded over a shared love of the Suffolk coastline. The two of them would sit in high, winged chairs and discuss with animation the towns of Aldeburgh and Southwold; they spoke of family holidays in cottages and caravans, the bitter taste of Adnams ale. It was on one such occasion, after a simple lunch and before their planned walk, that Jean realized she was going to marry him. Her first marriage had been agonized over, pinched and prodded until she was sure she was doing the right thing; but her second she decided upon without hesitation, while drinking a glass of red wine by the fire, her flushed cheeks reflected in its brass surround.

Two weeks later, Peter arrived home to find a suitcase packed in the hallway. She was sitting on the bottom step of the stairs already wearing her coat. 'We're going away,' she said. 'We're going on a magical mystery tour. Come on, get showered and changed. Quick, okay?'

She drove them both to a ramshackle cottage on the seafront at Aldeburgh. He loved its odd shape, its worn-down furnishings. They arrived late and he managed to sleep through till five or so. She woke with him and suggested they walked together down by the seafront.

'This is the perfect start to a day,' he said. 'If I could, I'd live by the sea. I'd walk by it every day.'

'We'll do that,' she said. 'One day we will do that.'

○

That evening she cooked his favourite meal of potted shrimp followed by steak and mashed potato. They could hear the waves as they ate, and both had appetites emboldened by the sea. In the lull before cheese and biscuits, she proposed to him just as she'd planned. In her right hand she held a velveteen box containing a simple engagement ring she'd bought from a flea market. She asked him to marry her, and he fell silent and wiped his mouth on a linen napkin. He sipped his wine and looked at the debris of the meal in front of him. His face, crumpled and with a small dab of sauce at the edge of his mouth, looked papery. He rapped his knuckles on the table. She felt her stomach plummet, as though she'd taken a jump from a diving board into a recently drained pool.

'Say something,' she said. 'Oh please, honey, say something at least.'

He wiped at his mouth again and put his head in his hands. He shook his head.

'No,' he said. 'I can't. I can't do that to you.'

'Do what?' she said.

'I can't,' he said. 'I promised myself I wouldn't do this.'

He looked away from her as he spoke. He told her he loved her very much. He told her that she had made him happier than he could ever have imagined. He told her that he never meant to let it get this far. He told her that she gave him hope and that there was nothing he would like to do more than marry her.

'So what is it? What?' she said. He looked up at her.

'I think I killed some people.'

○

It was the Thursday before the wedding, a little after three in the morning. Beside Jean, Peter slept peacefully. Since their engagement, decided upon after that long night in Aldeburgh, he had slept through every night. The night terrors – a

product not of genetics, but of genuine horror –
had disappeared, replaced by long dreamless
periods of sleep. He could not remember such
restfulness; she could not think of anything but
the dreams that now plagued her.

In the recurring nightmare, she saw bodies
blistered by heat, felt the air thick with the stench
of flesh and hair afire. The screams and the pleas
and the stretching arms, the metal melting on
belt buckles, shoes dissolving into the floor. And
him, her lover, watching, somehow flame retar-
dant and dressed in his suit, smoking a cigarette
lit from the inferno around him.

That Thursday she had been woken by it
again, the fifth time in the last three weeks, and
had been unable to rouse Peter or go back to sleep
herself. Jean looked at her fiancé, his breathing
easy and his body foetal. She put down the book
she had been looking at rather than reading, then
inched out of the bed. Pulling on a T-shirt with
No Problem written on the front – a present from
Jamaica – she moved into the hallway and then
down the stairs. They creaked as she descended,
but she no longer cared about waking him. Let
him wake, she thought, let him suffer too.

It was late summer and the air was close and muggy. She went into the kitchen and put on the kettle and opened the fridge. From a plastic container she took a block of cheese and cut a chunk off at an angle. The kettle boiled and she made tea, which she took through to the living room. Most nights she ended up there, sitting on the sofa, blue-lit by the television. She watched talk shows and documentaries and programmes signed for the deaf, whatever night-time fare she could find. These days, she knew so much about all manner of trivial things.

Jean turned on the television and lowered the volume. It was a nature documentary about the wildlife of Siberia. She blew on her tea and watched the programme until the commercial break. Her mug empty, she put it on the coffee table and got up from the deep red couch and started to rustle around inside the cushions of the armchair. Somewhere, in a hollow she'd fashioned inside the padding, there was a packet of cigarettes.

She'd taken to hiding her cigarettes in ever more elaborate, deceitful places; even though Peter didn't even know she had started smoking again. 'We have no secrets,' Peter was fond of saying, which she thought a stupid, idiotic thing to say: what he really meant was that the big secret was out and that the little ones didn't count. But for Jean the little secrets were the ones worth keeping. Which is why she hid the cigarettes with such ingenuity.

As she scrabbled around inside the chair, she began to hope that the packet wouldn't be there after all; that Peter had discovered them, torn them up, and thrown them away. When she found them she counted them out, even though she already knew precisely how many there were.

Jean walked through the lounge, opened the patio doors, and sat down on the folding canvas chair. She lit a cigarette and inhaled as much of the smoke as her lungs could take. She did this every night and often wondered whether she could die that way: asphyxiated by too much smoke taken too quickly into her lungs.

The night was still and calm. She flicked the ash from her cigarette into a small barbecue. Peter had bought it months before as a challenge to himself; but they'd only used it once. It had not been cleaned since and stubborn pieces of charred meat remained stuck to its grill. Every time she saw it, she thought she should clean it, but she never did. Some nights she was even tempted to pull some of the flesh off the metal and eat it. But she never did that either.

As she smoked, she tried not to think about the fire, nor think about Peter. She'd spent most of the nights since he'd told her thinking about it in one way or another. Sometimes simply recalling exactly what he'd said. Not the main part, not what he thought he'd done, but that first sentence that cracked and splintered her life. *I think I killed some people.*

She could hear the words crisply in her mind, recall the dampness of the rented cottage's rooms, see him sitting at the table, his hair well styled and his sweater well pressed and that dab of sauce still at the corner of his mouth. The softness of his voice, its soothing timbre saying something so brutal, so stark. *I think I killed some people.*

The more she thought of it, the more angry those six words made her. The non-specificity of *some people*, the prefacing of such unspeakable violence with *I think*. It made her want to shout and scream, to beat at his chest with her balled-up fists. You think you killed some people? You think?

Inevitably then she'd imagine the dead bodies, the ash of the living cremated, the fireball whoosh of the explosion. In those first months, she did a lot of research on the fire, research which, like the smoking, was another closely guarded secret. She read transcripts of firemen's testimonies, newspaper reports, the official governmental inquest. Nowhere was there blame attached; at no point did anyone say that there was someone culpable for the deaths of thirty-one people in a fire at King's Cross Underground station. But someone's fingers had dropped the match that had ignited the matter below the escalator steps. Someone was responsible.

She stood up and looked over the fence into next door's garden. It was neat and pretty, regimented flowers in beds and a well-maintained rockery. She wondered if they'd notice if she crept onto their lawn, lay down on the lush turf and slept. It was a strange idea and one that hung heavy in her head. She wanted to sleep; she wanted all the sleep he was denying her, but instead she took in another huge lungful of smoke.

On that evening, Peter had been drinking in a pub in Soho with his then girlfriend, Simone.

They were drunk and had argued over something and nothing. On the Underground their disagreements had become more personal. In front of an alarmed carriage, they had argued in her native French and later in English, his Galway accent increasingly loud. At Euston she ended their relationship and at King's Cross she danced past the crowds with Peter in pursuit. He lost her in the tunnels somewhere near the Piccadilly Line. He took the escalator and on the way up to the ticket hall struck a match, lit an Embassy and let the match fall. *I think I killed some people.* Thirty-one people to be precise. Jean even knew some of their names.

When his confession was at an end, she had, of course, told him not to be so stupid. In that rented cottage she'd taken him in her arms, her ring box still tight in her hand.

'Sshh,' she'd said. 'It's okay. I've got you. I've got you, Pete.' And she'd explained about how it could have been any number of people and that it was an accident just waiting to happen and that there was no possible way he could know it was him who had caused such a catastrophe. She felt starchy and nanny-like. She stroked his hair and could almost feel the relief flooding from him. They stayed like that for a long time, Jean telling him it wasn't his fault, that he wasn't to blame, that he was not responsible.

○

She watched next door's cat pad along the fence. For a moment she was tempted to flick her cigarette at it. She could see how easy it would be to hit its black and grey flank. The cat jumped down and still she had the cigarette poised, though now her shot was compromised. If she missed now, the cigarette would be lost in the tangle of weeds and nettles by the fence. It could start a fire. A real one, not the one that just burned up her nights. She had plenty of matches, she could set the whole lot alight and watch it go up, watch it rage from the upstairs bedroom, taking every garden with it.

She wished that he had never said anything. That the man she fell in love with was back; the shy, lonely person with a constant look of surprised happiness on his face. The killer of some people. Of thirty-one people. Absolved from that blame, he had become divorced from himself, and from her. Despite everything, she had preferred the remorse.

She put out her cigarette and looked back inside the still, dark house. Each night she watched for his bare ankles on the stairs, the look of horror on his face, his T-shirt and shorts damp with sweat. 'I had the dream again,' she'd hear him say, and she'd hold him and tell him that she'd got him and that he was safe. She wanted him to have the dreams again; she wanted him to take them back from her. But he never came down the stairs and never saw her smoking cigarettes sitting out on the canvas chair.

The cat stretched, sleek in the night, then washed itself for a time. When it stopped it nudged its nose against a stray piece of timber. Jean looked again at the matches and then back at the house. When she turned around again the cat was looking at her, holding her gaze with reflective, filmy eyes. It was still for a second, then darted off through the garden and out into safety.

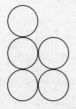

# *Lou Lou in the Blue Bottle*

It was all O'Neil's fault that I started running. Since I'd moved to New York, we'd quickly become close and were soon living together in a small Brooklyn apartment. Everything was fine until O'Neil decided to give up smoking. It was a snap decision, taken after he'd watched a television programme about an old man who'd had to have his leg amputated because of the cigarettes. O'Neil had explained his reasons and given me some unpleasant facts about what smoking does to the arteries. He asked me if I'd quit at the same time as a gesture of solidarity. I refused. I told him that I'd try to be as considerate as I could when I was at home, though.

He'd gone cold turkey: no patches, no gum,

just willpower. He'd done well, but his moods were even more erratic than normal. That morning he'd been smoke-free for two months. It was a Sunday and we were watching *The Rockford Files* and drinking coffee. He was unusually quiet and when I asked him if anything was wrong, he just grunted and pointed towards the television. I didn't say anything. Our friendship understood the importance of keeping quiet.

It was hot in the apartment; hot and dusky. We had a blackout screen covering the window to stop the sun shining directly into the room. Our place wasn't too big, just about large enough for the brown corduroy sofa we'd bought second-hand, a television set, stereo, coffee table and two bookshelves. We kept it clean and tidy – O'Neil had a crippling fear of rodent infestation – and illuminated it with low-wattage lamps. There were dun-coloured rugs covering the floorboards and above the television was a poster of Warhol's *Gold Marilyn*. O'Neil had taken an instant dislike to the picture when I'd put it up and asked me to take it down. We played paper-scissor-stone for it. Paper wraps stone, so Marilyn stayed where she was.

*The Rockford Files* finished and as I flipped

through the channels O'Neil tapped me on the arm.

'Rob,' he said. 'Can I ask you something?'

I nodded and kept my eye on the television.

'Do you think I need to lose weight?'

I paused and put down the remote control. I looked at his apple cheeks, his chest and gut, his ham-hock legs.

'Of course not,' I said and threw a cushion at him. He screwed up his face, almost as though I'd caught him unawares. But he looked downcast. My smile, so quickly reached for, slackened. I felt something shift in the room, like the blocked-out sun had passed behind a cloud.

'Jesus, are you serious?' I said. 'I mean—'

'Of course I'm serious,' he cut in. 'I wouldn't ask if I wasn't serious, would I?'

I finished my coffee and stubbed out my cigarette. It joined the others: an orange question mark in an I ❤ NY ashtray. There was sweat gathering at O'Neil's brow.

'Come on, Rob. It's a simple question. Do I need to shed some pounds or what?'

'No,' I said. 'Of course you don't.'

Realistically he could have dropped three stone

and still have been overweight. But since we'd been friends I'd never known him to have a problem with how he looked. Other big people were conscious of their weight, the rolls that would appear when seated. Not O'Neil. He constantly drew attention to his body, rubbing his belly as though petting a kitten, pulling at his jowls, and massaging his wattle. His body language, his movements, his very essence was defined by this hulking, jellied frame.

'Seriously?' he said. It was difficult to tell whether he was relieved. I could hear his breath over the television.

'Seriously,' I said and leant back into the couch.

He shook his head: 'You fucking liar.'

With a bit of effort, O'Neil got up from the sofa. He shucked off his Batman T-shirt to reveal a pair of scantily haired breasts, two bloated nipples, and a perfectly round, pendulous belly.

'You think I don't know?' he said. 'You think I can't see?' He held the T-shirt in his hand like a burning flag. I turned away.

'Rob, look at me,' he said and slapped his stomach, the fat rippling, his pectorals giggling in its wake.

I looked up at my half-naked best friend. Slowly a smile took shape across his mouth. His lips were fleshy and wide for his face; the dimples in his cheeks making him seem childlike. He started to laugh, and I laughed too. His eyes were bloodshot; he'd not been sleeping well.

O'Neil put his T-shirt back on and collapsed into the sofa. We went back to watching the television. *Murder, She Wrote*. When it was over, I touched him lightly on the arm.

'If you really do want to lose some weight, I don't mind helping,' I said.

O'Neil cracked a long, contagious smile, as warm as the room and just as comforting.

'That's why you'll always be my bitch, Robert Wilkinson,' he said. 'You always know exactly the right thing to say.'

○

Two days later, dressed in sweatpants and sweatshirts, the two of us wandered the streets of Brooklyn on the way to the gym O'Neil's uncle owned. It was a twenty-minute walk through shit-smeared sidewalks and gutters bearded with spent crack vials. The concrete walls and reinforced grilles of the shops were heavy with graffiti.

Spindly men and women hung around doorways and the spaces by dumpsters. Two cop cars drove past, both with their lights and sirens turned off. When the third passed by, I began to regret that I'd offered to help. Sportswear has never become me and I couldn't imagine dying dressed like that: an eternity decked out in Nike, Adidas and Fila.

'I haven't been round here in years,' O'Neil said, his face shrouded by his hooded sweatshirt. I kept my head down, uncomfortably snug in the soft cotton. In the middle distance, the sign for Charlie's Gym swung back and forth. O'Neil pointed it out with enthusiasm.

'This is going to be great, Rob,' he said, then paused. His hood still up, he leant down to me. 'Thanks,' he said, 'I appreciate this, I really do.'

○

Charlie's Gym was above a second-hand electrical goods shop. O'Neil and I went up the back stairs, the smell of piss and disinfectant violent at the bottom, changing to a more general body smell the closer we got to the gym itself.

O'Neil pushed open the door into a pigeon-grey space illuminated by harsh strip lighting.

In the centre was a ring where Charlie was training a young black kid. Charlie held a pair of focus
gloves up and away from his face and the kid
was smashing his fists into them. We watched
him punch as we wandered past a knot of ripped,
tattooed men, working dumb-bells like lifers. No
one spoke to us, but the light rain of skipping, the
grunting abuse of the focus gloves and the shuffle
of feet was ample distraction from their silence.

Charlie called break and O'Neil held up his
arm.

'Uncle Charlie!'

'Jackie!' he said and clambered out of the ring.
'So you're finally here, eh? Finally you wanna lose
these guts, right?' He was laughing and holding
O'Neil's rolls of fat in his hands. O'Neil laughed
and raised an eyebrow at me.

'You're going to be in a whole world of pain for
weeks, you know that? You ready for it?' O'Neil
was on the balls of his feet and already dancing.

'I am, Uncle Charlie,' he said as he aimed a
comic punch at his temple. 'I wanna be a champion not a chump.'

'Good man,' he said and then the two of them
stopped jabbing and dancing and sparring. Charlie

was taller than I expected, better looking. He was in his late fifties, lithe, with an impressive musculature and sharp black eyes. He looked at me then. If he'd worn glasses he'd have peered over the top of them.

'Who's this?' he said to O'Neil.

'This is my good friend Robert Wilkinson,' O'Neil said. 'He's from England.'

Charlie nodded toward me and held out his hand. 'Nice to meet you.'

His grip started out limp then got stronger, like he was playing peanuts. His face turned red and I laughed. Eventually he released me.

'With that hair,' he said, 'you look like a little girl, you know that?'

○

Charlie was serious about O'Neil's programme. He'd clearly given it a lot of thought. I wouldn't have thought that getting O'Neil lifting weights would help him lose weight, but I wasn't the one who'd owned a gym for twenty years. The first part of the routine was skipping. Charlie showed us both how to do it properly. After my fifth attempt ended with me almost flat on my back, Charlie stopped me.

'Your heart's just not in this, is it?' he said. He said it kindly enough, though it was hard not to sense that I'd let him down. O'Neil kept going.

'I'm just not that coordinated, that's all. I find things like this hard work.'

'I can see that.'

'I'm only really here to help O'Neil,' I said, leaning in closer to him. 'You know, show him some support. Help him lose some weight.'

'That's good that you're looking out for my nephew. It's good, but I can't have you hanging around in my gym not training. This place' – he shrugged – 'has got rules. Boxing's all about discipline. I don't let my boys cuss in this gym. My word is law. This place is a temple, you understand? So when I say you train, you train, all right?'

I nodded and looked around for anything requiring minimum coordination. In the corner was a machine covered with a sheet of tarpaulin. I pointed to it.

'Is that a treadmill?' I asked. Charlie squinted.

'Yes, son, I believe it is.'

'Can I train on that?'

His shoulders dropped and his weight shifted to the balls of his feet. Charlie looked at O'Neil, then at me.

'I don't think it works,' he said eventually.

'Really?'

'I don't know. You get it to work, you can use it.'

O'Neil came over then, glistening and beetroot-red. Charlie pushed a pair of practice gloves into his stomach.

'Now you're going to hit this bag just as I tell you,' he said, moving us over to the next station. O'Neil made to ask for a break to regain his breath, but Charlie shot him a look that not even the heavyweight champion of the world would have dared contradict.

I watched O'Neil intently from the other side of the bag. At first his combinations were tired and laboured, but then he began to grasp what he was supposed to be doing. The power in his shoulders was incredible. It looked like he was trying to stick his fists through the padding.

'Right-left-right. Upper cut. Jab. Jab. And relax,' Charlie called and O'Neil responded. Sweat was dripping off him, his arms slick and tensed.

He seemed to be enjoying it. I could barely recognize my best friend in the arms, fist and stance of the man hitting the bag.

'Left-right-jab-jab-upper-cut.' O'Neil hammered the bag again. It was too much. I wandered over to the treadmill, took off its wrapper and pressed some buttons. I looked down and followed the power cord to the wall and flicked the switch. There were beeps and flashes. I waited for it to settle then got on the track. I was still playing with buttons when someone grabbed me by the scruff of my Ramones T-shirt.

'What the fuck d'you think you doing?' the man said. His neck muscles were strained, steely like the spokes of an umbrella. He was a guy in his forties with dark, dark skin. He wore an LA Lakers vest.

The man was snorting with rage, and I tried to wrestle away from him. But soon Charlie was on him. I didn't catch what Charlie said, but the Lakers fan apologized straight away, then headed towards the medicine balls.

'You okay?' Charlie said once I'd started walking on the treadmill.

'Fine,' I said. 'What was that all about?'

'That's enough walking, friend,' he said with a smile. 'Time to run.' He pressed the pace button several times, taking me from comfort to pain in a matter of seconds. Charlie laughed as I tried to keep up with the rubber track. Eventually I managed to get the speed back to a level with which I could cope, and settled into a light jog, coughing and hoping I wouldn't puke on Uncle Charlie's floor.

Considering the years of inactivity, my body reacted better than I had expected. I wasn't going too quickly, but I was steady on my feet. Keeping a constant speed, I watched a sparring contest in the ring, saw a guy drop some powder into a drink, another man spotting for a bench press which looked impossible (he lifted it on the third attempt). And then, as I looked at my shoes, I felt something swell inside of me, like something was opening and all my body's molecules were splitting apart. I felt light, unencumbered, as though everything extraneous to the act of running had been erased. I pushed the speedometer up a couple of notches. And kept to a beat. I felt like I could – no, that I should – run for ever. And then I saw her face, alive and ahead of me.

She was smiling, beckoning me to follow her. She looked the same as she had the day she'd died, her hair tied up in a bun, no make-up, dressed simply in jeans and T-shirt. For a moment she seemed so close that I could smell her perfume – Lou Lou in the blue bottle – but then Charlie came over and pressed stop on the machine. I didn't know where to look.

'That's a good first session, boys. Well done,' Charlie said. 'Now if you two want to shower upstairs at my place' – he threw O'Neil a set of keys with a gold boxing glove fob – 'I'll be up in a little while. Make yourselves comfortable. There's beers in the refrigerator.'

He picked up his focus pads and climbed back into the ring where another heavily tattooed man was waiting for him. I could hear the thudding impacts even in the stairwell.

○

I expected Charlie's place to be a shrine to boxing, a museum of signed photos and fight posters, old gloves and imitation belts with gluey fake stones. Instead it was a strangely feminized space that had been left to moulder. There were scatter cushions on the comfortable-looking divan. There was a gingham tablecloth on the dining table and a bead curtain separating the kitchen from the lounge. On the coffee table was a vase with some dead flowers inside. The floor needed sweeping and there was dust on the television set. On the wall were three watercolours of Paris. They were amateurish; and I wondered if Uncle Charlie had painted them himself. Tough guys always make shitty painters.

The only piece of boxing memorabilia I could find was in the bathroom. It was a framed *Esquire* cover from 1968: Muhammad Ali bleeding from various arrow wounds. There was condensation on the glass from O'Neil's shower. I wiped it away, showered, then towelled myself dry. I put on my sweatshirt and sweatpants and went back into the living room. O'Neil was on his second bottle of beer.

'Boxing makes me thirsty.'

'Breathing makes you thirsty,' I said helping myself to a beer.

'Ain't that the truth,' O'Neil said.

○

After a dinner of steak, green beans, broccoli and spinach, O'Neil fell asleep on the divan. Charlie and I sat at the table: we'd moved on to bourbon and he was recounting stories of the fight game that meant nothing to me. He'd ask me whether I'd heard of a fighter and I'd say no and he'd go on to tell me all about him anyway. He was a good storyteller — the kind who would make friends in any bar in any country of the world. As he shovelled some ice into my glass, I remembered the man who'd come for me on the treadmill.

'What was that guy's problem? The one in the Lakers vest.' Charlie paused and then poured out the drinks. He placed the glass in front of me and took a long sip of his whiskey.

'It's complicated,' he said. 'I'm sorry. It's my fault.'

'The guy nearly knocked me out.'

He nodded. 'You know something, Robert. It sometimes seems to me that we're the unluckiest family in the whole goddamned world,' he said. 'It's like death and bad luck are lying in wait for us all the time. O'Neil's told you about his sister, Gloria, right?'

I nodded.

'Well, everything went to hell that day and nothing's come back. Even things that seem good one minute, always go wrong soon after. It's like since that gangbanger shot her, we've been cursed or something.'

'So why did that guy want to rip my head off?' I said. 'Was it to do with Gloria?'

He shook his head.

'You ever been in love?' he said.

I said nothing. I thought of Helen's body in the smashed car, the blood.

'I fell in love with a woman fifteen years younger than me,' he said, not waiting for me to answer. 'And she fell for me too. For other people that would be the start of something, wouldn't it? A heatwave in the autumn of life' – he smiled and shook his head, the smoke pooling around him – 'but that wasn't ever on the undercard. The guy with the Lakers vest is her brother. The whole thing just freaked him out.'

I looked at the table and fingered the cork placemat.

'You don't have to tell me,' I said.

'I want to tell you.'

'Don't tell me. It's not worth it.'

He picked up the bottle of Jim Beam and poured us two more healthy shots. O'Neil grunted and shifted his bulk on the couch. Charlie steepled his hands and said: 'She was the most beautiful woman in the whole world.' It was the perfect sentence to start a late night confession.

○

'She really was, you know? People say that about people all the time, I know, but it's true. I've been all over this country, seen most of the states, but I've never seen a woman as beautiful as Leona. She was so beautiful that to me she looked like what every other woman had been practising at becoming for the past two thousand years.'

He took a picture from his wallet and pitched it across the table. It was a Polaroid, smudgy and battered. Leona was standing outside Charlie's gym, smiling, late afternoon sunlight glowing around her. Despite the casual track pants and the UCLA sweatshirt, she looked elegant. High cheekbones led down to a mouth filled with prominent white teeth, gold hoop earrings contrasting with her dark skin. She looked a bit like an older version of Lisa Bonet. I passed the photo back and he carefully replaced it inside his wallet.

'We met in the market of all places. Just up the street from here. She was buying tomato sauce and I wasn't looking where I was going. Our carts crashed into one another. She asked if she knew me because I sure looked familiar. And then I remembered I'd seen her before but only from when she picked up her brother from the gym. She laughed and said, "Of course! You're Mr O'Neil. My brother talks about you all the time. Says you've got a story for every occasion."

'I must have coloured at that, 'cause she laughed again. I tried to smile but I guess it came out like a grimace, maybe, or bad stomach acid.

'"I think that's cool," she says then. "I like people who can tell a good story."'

Charlie let out a long sigh.

'You see, son, I've spent my whole life around men. All of it. In the ring, in the gym, in the car on the way to the next fight. I mean I've not spent much time in the company of women. And I don't mean that in a queer way. It's just that I've never really *got* women. I just wasn't at the races. In the ring you see a punch, you block it or you get out of the way or you take the punch. Simple. Black and white. With women I never found that. I've had women, but never for very long. Give me a wild kid from the Bronx ripped on 'roids and rage and I can do something about it. Show me an attractive woman and I'm looking for the nearest exit.'

He took a long sip of whiskey and made a fist with his right hand.

'But that day, in the market, standing next to this beautiful woman with two cans of tomato sauce in her hands, somehow I grew some real *cojones*, y'know what I mean? Some proper balls. So I turns to her and says: "If you like stories, maybe I can tell you some over a cup of coffee some time?"

'She looks me up and down and says: "So long as I can get a donut too."

'I couldn't believe it. We met an hour later and we drank coffee and ate donuts. Leona ends up telling me all about her life and I just listen, soaking up her voice like it was pure gravy. She'd come to New York from LA when she was sixteen. She'd always meant to go back, but New York kept finding new ways of keeping her occupied. She worked as a clerk in a bank in Manhattan and loved riding the subway. I liked the way she touched her hair as she spoke. I told her some of my better fight stories and her eyes dazzled as I told them. She said she loved tales of the old boxers.

'"These new guys," she says to me after I told her a story about Sugar Ray Robinson, "they're not real fighters. They're like machines with muscles, or something. It's like they're wearing battle suits. Gimme the old guys any day." I couldn't speak for about a minute. I was expecting Allen Funt from *Candid Camera* to step through the door. She was perfect. Perfect in every way.

'I saw her the next week. We met for coffee again. She asks me if I'd like to come round to hers for dinner. I didn't know what to say. I couldn't understand what a thirty-five-year-old black woman would want to do with an old fool like me. She apologized and we sat and watched our coffees go cold.

'"Is there something wrong?" she says. "I thought we were getting on real well."

'And I say, "Sure," and then give her a compliment.

'"So, are you afraid of my cooking? You

expecting polk salad and chitlins and molasses?"
she says to me just like that. And I start mum-
bling, that it's not that at all.

'She puts her hand on mine then and starts
saying about how age and all the rest of it means
nothing to her. She likes me, is all. Likes my
gentle hands and my muscles and the way I bob
my head as I speak. Then she kisses me. The next
day I go round to her place for dinner. Six weeks
later she's moved her stuff in here and she's talking about redecoration.'

Charlie paused and went to refill the glasses.

'I don't need to go into all the details. They're
not important. All you need to know is that I was
the happiest I've ever been. It was like something
out of dreams, or off the movies or something. It
was like we were fused together. We understood
each other so well we didn't need to communicate.
We were just so happy that it seemed nothing bad
could ever happen to anyone.'

He laughed then and looked longingly for a
moment at my cigarettes.

'The only punch you never see is the one that
puts you on the canvas. You can't ever see that one
coming, that's what they say. About three years

ago, things became a little strained, somehow not quite as special. And it hit Leona real hard. She couldn't understand it, couldn't get herself excited about anything. She stopped coming to the fights, stopped making dinner. She just watched television and cried sometimes in the night. It was strange. It was like someone had thrown water on a fire. She just seemed to run out of spark.

'She was usually so active, but now she just wanted to stay home. She'd look at me with those beautiful eyes when I got home and she'd say: "I'm losing you. I don't want to, but I'm losing you." And I didn't know what else to say but: "No. No, you're not losing me."

'This went on for a few months. She would read these books with titles like *You Can Change Your Life* and *The Seven Stages of Success and Happiness*. Y'know that kind of Oprah stuff? They did nothing and she'd throw them across the room after just a few pages. "These people know nothing, Charlie," she'd say, "they don't have a clue how bad it feels." One day I came home and she'd been drinking. She spent two whole days throwing up. A month later, I said she should go and see a doctor.

'I could tell she wasn't sure about the idea, but she went along. And the doctor says to her to go and see this other guy, an analyst. So I take her to see this analyst, hoping that everything'll work itself out. She's in there for an hour or so and comes out like she's been sparring with Max Schmeling. On the way home she tells me that she talked for all that time, but nothing seemed to make any sense. And then she starts to laugh. She laughs and says, "You know what this crazy man wants me to do? What's going to fix my broken head? You ready for this, Charlie? Running!" She starts laughing even more. "All this time and all I needed was to do myself some jogging!"

'I went to see the shrink. He was a tall woolly headed guy. Still, he looked kind enough. Not a crank at least. I waited for him to finish his meetings then followed him out to the parking lot. I told him what was happening and if there was anything I should be doing. He looked at me for a time and said all that usual stuff about patient confidentiality. Then he held my shoulder and said, "Get her running." I thought maybe it was time to get a different analyst.

'But after I left him, I thought maybe it was worth a shot. So I got her a treadmill and set it up in the gym. She looked at me like I was insane. "Charlie," she said to me, "that guy's crazy. Running isn't going to make me any better." I just told her to do it for me. I put the machine in the corner of the gym so she could watch me as she ran and took her down to a specialist running store and bought her running pants and some shoes. I think she knew how hard it was for me too.

'For the first two days I was treading on eggshells around her. Her sadness was filling up the apartment. It was like it was drowning us both. But she put on the jogging suit and the shoes and did two miles the first day, two miles the second, then three miles on the third. On the fourth day we could feel it come back. It was like a homecoming.

'"That doctor ain't so crazy after all," I said. And she kissed me like she had that first time.

'Every day she'd come home from work, change and come join me in the gym. She'd run for as long as I'd train, then we'd have dinner. It was like the old times again. It was perfect.'

He was shaking slightly now.

'Feels like I've been talking for ever.' He finished his drink then went to the kitchen and filled up a kettle for coffee.

'It was like that for a few months,' he went on. 'Better than ever. Then Leona started to lose weight. At first it was gradual, but then it was hard to ignore. I reckon she dropped maybe twenty-four pounds in about one month. I couldn't understand it; but she was so happy there wasn't any point in saying anything. She was eating, I knew that because I was watching her. In fact she was eating all the time. I started putting protein supplements in her food, but it wasn't doing any good. She just got thinner and thinner. She was wasting away in front of me, but she wouldn't have me call a doctor. "Charlie," she'd say, "I'm fine, honey. You always liked your fighters lean, didn't you?"

'The happiness of those months disappeared as quick as her chest and her ass. When she wasn't running she was thinking about it. I could tell. It's like when fighters have been hit so hard they can't hear, but they're still nodding their heads, pretending they understand the instructions.

'One night I woke up. It was three-thirty in the

morning and Leona wasn't in bed. She wasn't in the apartment either so I unlocked the door and went down into the gym. The lights were off, but I could hear a noise inside. I called out and heard this scraping, falling sound. I pushed on the light and Leona was lying in a heap by the running machine. I ran over to her and scooped her up, then called for an ambulance. She was barely conscious when they took her in.

'Next day she was awake and lucid. I held her hand.

'"I'm sorry, Charlie. I'm sorry," she kept saying over and over again. Apparently it had been going on for months. "There was something there," she says to me one night, "I could see us together where no one could hurt us, where we were forever like we were before. All I had to do was keep running. If I kept running I knew we were both safe."

'The doctors reckoned she'd been running well over a hundred and fifty miles a week, most of them late at night while I was sleeping. Her body eventually just gave out. Just like that.'

He clicked his finger and took the whistling kettle from the stove.

'I'm so sorry,' I said. He made the coffee and handed me a mug.

'I see her every day at the hospital, but she looks through me. "I used to love you, didn't I?" she says sometimes when I see her. "But I could never run far enough, could I? If I could run for ever, I'd find you again."

'They don't think she'll ever come back. It's in the blood, apparently. Her aunt's locked up in San Diego, convinced that Nixon's put out a hit on her. Her grandfather went crazy too, in the war, poor bastard.'

He blew on his mug of coffee. 'Now isn't that the saddest thing you've ever heard?' he said and gave out a low laugh. I thought of Helen's body in the smashed car, the blood, Lou Lou in the blue bottle. We drank in silence, then O'Neil woke up, looking confused like it wasn't the room he was expecting. He looked at the clock and then at his watch. It was late.

'We should be making a move, Rob,' he said. 'We got meetings first thing.'

'Thanks, Charlie,' I said.

'Yeah, thanks, Uncle Charlie.'

'It's my pleasure. See you boys soon, I hope,' Charlie said.

'Tomorrow,' I said. 'We'll see you tomorrow.'

*Eclipse*

Our baby cries, so I put him to my breast; his mouth greedy like his father. He is seven months old, but will not take to the bottle: instead he clings to me. Sometimes I wonder if it will ever end, and imagine him a grown man with sharp teeth biting on my sore-swollen nipples; and this makes me both laugh and shiver. He has his father's face then, the same eyes that hooked me the first time.

Everything now smells of spilled milk, talcum powder and nappies. This is what he tells me, and I believe him; though since the birth I've not caught the scent of anything at all. He could have started smoking again for all I know – the decision to quit was his and his alone – or he could have stopped washing. Or he could be coming home night after night smelling strongly of his lover. He could stink of her sweat and her perfume. His breath could hum with the taste of her and I wouldn't know. Maybe this is some kind of trade-off: my son for one of my senses.

○

He fell in love with her on the 15th of September. This was almost exactly two months before I fell pregnant. How I knew, I can't say. It just flashed before me, like ticker tape, as he took a bottle of wine from the fridge: he has fallen deeply, madly in love. That radiance you get when pregnant is nothing to the sheen that comes with such passion and devotion. It burned through him like an eclipse: beautiful, but dangerous to look upon.

○

The desire for motherhood came to me by stealth; for years I'd had no maternal feelings at all, preferring the company of cats to children. Mal seemed happy with this. But as children proliferated around us, our friends succumbing one by one, I couldn't quite fight the tugging inside, the slight hesitation as I passed back babies to their beaming parents. When I decided, I was thirty-nine; Mal thirty-five. It was not something we discussed. Instead I threw away my contraceptive pills and got us started that very afternoon.

We had been trying for six months; a half year of thermometers, cycles and bored, routine sex. After he found her though, things were different. The sex became more urgent and insistent, almost cruel. I was under no illusions: I knew that each time we fucked he was thinking of her. Once, he put his finger up my arse and moved it up and down in a way he'd never done before. It was something she liked and any pleasure it provoked collapsed as I imagined her underneath him, his fingers inside her.

We only managed to conceive because he was in love with that woman. I'm convinced of that.

○

I met her once, at a leaving party. Mal's boss was retiring and the whole work crowd were drinking in Vodka Revolution. When I arrived he was talking to her and another woman. I knew which one she was. She had long dark hair, a large nose, and her breasts were pushed up inside her T-shirted chest. She looked intelligent; her skin pale and flawless, her eyebrows in need of tweezing. Mal saw me and did not flinch, introducing the two women as Libby and Teri. They had been working on a project with Mal and a few others. I shook both their hands; hers was cool to the touch.

'Mal's got the untidiest desk in the whole office,' Teri said. 'He must be a nightmare at home.' Libby gazed at the floor and then started looking through her large, green handbag.

'His mum still calls him Messy Mal,' I said. 'She says she's never met anyone like him, and she's got six kids, so she should know.'

Mal laughed and shook his head.

'Don't believe a word of it. I've been house-trained now,' he said. 'I even take my shoes off when I get in.'

Libby stood. 'I'm going out for a smoke. Anyone care to join me?' she said.

We shook our heads and she sighed.

'Everyone's a quitter these days, aren't they?' she said. 'Lovely to meet you, Elaine, catch you all in a bit.' She got up and brushed past me. I caught a brief note of her perfume; something plummy,

cinnamon-like, probably expensive. When I imagine what he smells like now, that's what comes to
mind.

○

There is no evidence for the affair. I have yet to
find lipstick traces, letters, emails or texts. The
phone does not ring at odd times of night. There
have been no suspicious wrong numbers. He acts
in much the same way as usual; quiet, messy Mal
with his books spread out over the kitchen table,
catching up on paperwork, opening the wine. But
I see it. I know it's there.

Back when my stomach began to swell, my son
growing inside, I wondered how Mal was coping.
He had not really considered the fact that we
would actually have a child, I'm sure of that. The
months of trying had convinced him that there
was fault with one or both of us. At night I would
watch him sleep and hate him for seeming not to
care. I'd hear him snore and snuffle and feel a
sharp, splitting pain in my shoulder and in my
breast. I would get up then and go down to the
kitchen. As the sun came up, I would make tea
and sip it sitting at the kitchen table, its top still
covered with his books and papers.

I didn't know how he could bear to spend his nights and days away from her. When I first met Mal, I'd not wanted to spend a single moment apart from him. I'd gone to football games and watched horror movies, I'd driven him to places he'd never been before, places he'd always wanted to visit. I did anything I could to be with him.

On a bright November afternoon, we walked around Chartwell House, Mal talking about Churchill's depression while I nodded and told him that I was interested, honestly. He held my hand as we sat by the lake and then we kissed in a way that felt like reinvention. Even now I remember those kisses with clarity, and wonder if they felt the same in his mouth as they did in mine. Being in love can be a solitary business I've always thought: you can only get so close, and no further. Those barriers can't be broken, no matter how much you love someone.

When I was heavily pregnant, I asked Mal about that afternoon at Chartwell and he said how much he would like to go back, that there was a new exhibition he'd be interested to see. He did not mention the lake, or the kisses, or that we'd stopped off on the way home to make love in a secluded field. Do those kisses only exist for me now? Do her kisses linger? Are they the ones that come back to surprise him?

○

Zachary looks up, milk escaping from his mouth. They are probably together now. He is supposed to be watching football at the pub, but he could easily be with her. He could be there crying, telling her that he wants to be with her, that his heart aches and his hands shake, but that he can't just walk out: not now. I can see her big nose, her tear-struck face. 'I love you,' she says. 'Why is this so difficult? Why can't life be simple?' And then they collapse on the bed and make hurried, angry love. He puts his finger up her arse and moves it up and down. She tells him she loves him as he climaxes.

○

I burp Zach and move about the lounge, the radio playing in the background. When I was a teen-ager, before I cut my hair and started smoking and fooling around with boys, I used to listen to a radio show in which a DJ read out people's true love stories. His voice was consistently sombre and listeners were unable to tell whether that day's instalment would end happily or bring a tear to their eye. I'd always wanted to have my epic affair read out to the nation, the soundtrack to a million coffee breaks; but that was a long time ago now. Now it was a different story, and hardly the one I had imagined.

The love story still features me, but I am no longer the star. I am the woman unnamed; the one for whom you do not root. At the centre of the stage there is now my husband and his lover. They are soulmates, and they would be together were it not for the child — a child that he loves and understands is vastly more important than his own needs. The story goes on like this for years, the two of them breaking off the affair then finding each other later, desperate for each other's embrace. In this telling of the story, he stays home to look after the baby, while I go out to work. He is a good father, but he cannot help but pine for his soulmate.

In the love story I am just a shadow, a blip on their perfect romance. After five years? Six? However long, eventually Mal confesses. He tells the story of the perfect romance and I, the blip and shadow, am quiet and thankful that he has been honest and a good father to Zachary. He leaves that day and goes to live with the woman he fell in love with on the 15th of September. At the end of the story the DJ sermonizes, adding a conclusion that reminds listeners that sometimes it's better to have things out in the open, rather than living a lie. Stale homily wisdom served up as fresh advice, followed by the opening mournful bars of their song: 'Dark End of the Street'.

○

The story the DJ does not tell is the story of a woman who loves her husband with the same passion with which he loves his mistress. It is the story of her love for her child, the only positive thing to come from this fractured relationship. And for as long as this child is young, his father will be around, attentive and dedicated. His lover may have his heart and his mind and his constant thoughts, but she will not have him. Not in the way that she wants and needs him. Not in the way that he wants and needs her. They can have their song, and their grand passion, but I will always be there, mother and wife both. Why should I not break his heart the way he has broken mine?

○

The radio goes to a news bulletin and a female voice reads the stories in this order: war, famine, freak weather, murder, political scandal and then the weather. The door opens and Mal is there, slightly red at the cheeks and wearing his old duffel coat.

'Hey, love,' he says. 'Is he asleep?'

'Yes,' I say.

He puts his arm around me and kisses me on the cheek, then on the lips. He smiles, takes off his coat and goes to the kitchen. I follow him there.

'What was the score?' I ask.

'Two all. It was a good game, too,' he says. 'Neil sends his love.'

He could have checked the scores on his phone on the way home, and Neil would do anything for Mal. He takes a beer from the fridge.

'Has he been okay?' he says. 'Not too grizzly?'

'He's been fine,' I say, 'gorgeous.' And I look at Mal for hints of make-up, glitter, evidence of her. I cuddle up to him.

'I love you,' I say.

'I love you too,' he says, but too quickly. I put my cheek next to his and breathe in through my nose as much as I can. There is nothing, not even a breath. And then, for a moment, I think I can smell cinnamon and plums, and her, and then cigarettes, and then beer, and then just the smell of the outside world.

*Real Work*

You had a theory that heaven is the constant repetition of the happiest moment of your life. For you, this was experienced on a bus heading to meet your first boyfriend; an older man with a wife and infant daughter. You said it was the first time you'd done something deliberately wrong, and your young heart beat like it never had before, and never has since.

For me, it was the morning after we first met. You were sleeping and I was watching the dawn spread a deep, burning orange over the East End. I was in your living room, on the fifteenth storey of a crumbling sixties council block, and on the turntable 'Angie' by the Rolling Stones was playing. The window was open, there was a warm breeze, and as I walked out onto the small balcony I smoked one of your imported American cigarettes. Below me the city was waking, but was still groggy. I could see the stained dome of St Paul's, the suggestive lights of Canary Wharf and for the first time I saw a silent beauty in those buildings. Jagger sang to a quiet, cowed city, and if it hadn't been for the scent of you on my skin, I'd have thought myself utterly alone in the world.

○

You said that you were sick of dating artists; their complex emotional needs, their conflicted egos. We were sitting at a booth in a mock-1950s diner in Soho, drinking milkshakes and sharing fries. You had put bourbon in the drinks and were toying with a paper napkin. It was our fifth date. Two bald men walked past us arm in arm, then stopped to kiss. You noticed the look on my face and for a moment I thought you were going to mock my prudishness. But you didn't and instead balled up the napkin and told me to hurry because we were going to meet Mary.

It was summertime, early evening, and the sky was darkening. You were dressed in a black and white smock dress and had recently dyed your hair a shocking platinum blonde. We lit cigarettes and smoked them as we walked the litter-swept streets. By the Raymond Revue Bar we kissed and with a pinch of my behind, you pushed me through the multicoloured ribbons hanging from a sex shop doorway. I had never been inside a sex shop before and I didn't know where to look. You picked up a vibrator and waved it at me. You laughed. Behind the counter, the attendant was asleep. You left a pile of coins on the counter and took a vial of poppers.

I asked you what they were for. You narrowed your eyes.

'This isn't a put-on, is it?' you said. 'I mean the way you are . . . sometimes it's like you're straight off the boat or something.'

'I'm just a clean-living country boy with fine morals,' I said.

'We'll soon see about that,' you said and took me by the hand.

○

Mary ran a domination studio on the third floor ofa residential block just behind Beak Street. She had a heaving bosom and a tattooed tear just below her right eye. You knew her from art college. While you were in the bathroom, Mary showed me an adult diaper, a gimp mask and a variety of nipple clamps. She was trying to shock me, but I tried to remain impassive. I asked Mary how she conducted her taxes. I was serious, but you both found it most amusing. Mary said that the majority of the men who came to visit her were like me: timid, fragile and confused. I asked what the most popular request was for. She paused for a moment. 'It used to be the lash,' she said, 'but now it's crushing. They like me to lie on them until they can hardly breathe. Kinky buggers love it.'

She stood then and picked up a black patent clutch bag. 'Would you like me to crush you?' she said. 'Would you like me to give you a good old crushing?' I must have looked terrified because you both laughed again.

'Oh no, Mary,' you said. 'This one's crushed enough.'

○

'So, what's she like, then?' Tom said. I hadn't seen him in over three weeks and had been avoiding his calls. We were in the back room of the Faltering Fullback, the place we always met.

I hadn't wanted to come, but he had insisted and besides, you said you needed a night just for you. There were things you needed to do.

'She's different,' I said. 'She reminds me a bit of Helen Dyer from school. You remember her?'

'The Goth?'

'She wasn't a Goth. She was an artist.'

'So she's an artist, this Cara?'

'Trying to be.'

'Tall? Short? Fat? Skinny?'

'Hard to describe.'

'Hard to describe, how?' Tom said.

'Tallish, sort of curvy,' I said, trying to imagine how you would describe yourself. 'She likes old clothes, fifties stuff mainly. She wears glasses. She's into art and politics and culture. She's passionate.'

Tom took a long pull on his beer and rested his head on his meaty hand. 'So have you?'

'Yes. But don't ask me for details.'

Tom smiled and scratched his beard. 'I can't wait to meet her.'

I nodded and lit a cigarette. The adverts finished and the second half of the football began. The number 14 challenged the number 6, his studs raised and his feet high. Number 6 collapsed and the pub was furious.

'That's a fucking yellow if ever I've seen it,' Tom said. 'That fucker's an animal.'

○

Cities are as big or as small as you wish to make them. Before I met you, mine was approximately one and a half square miles. I had a house in South Tottenham and worked for Haringey Council in Wood Green. If I went out, say to meet Tom, it was within these parameters. You did not know either of these areas and were not much taken with them on the few occasions you visited.

Instead you showed me all the places you had lived, districts full of grotty bedsitters and shared houses, squats and tenements. In Brixton, in Harlow, in Peckham and New Cross; in Hackney, in Kensal Rise, in Kentish Town, in Finchley, in Gospel Oak and on the Edgware Road. You'd lived north, east, south, and west and all points in between. You moved on a whim, trying to find the perfect place to call your home.

'I love this city,' you said one evening as we

took a taxi across town. 'It's a visceral feeling, you know? Like it's tearing at my insides.' The street lamps and neon bled through the taxi windows. 'I love it like I love you.'

You took it upon yourself to expand my confined city. Early on Sunday mornings, you took me into the silent financial district. In the calm, as day broke, you'd point out architecture and talk of chaos theory, radical Marxism, fiscal inequalities. You introduced me to vegan cafes, Vietnamese canteens, Turkish grill houses and Albanian tea rooms. You took me shopping on Cheshire Street to buy clothes that didn't embarrass you. I liked the way you looked at me wearing them, and the way you put your arm in mine as we walked.

We went out most nights. On the weekends we would sleep in late and only leave your place when it was dark. We'd meet your friends. So many friends. They were not the kind of people I would ordinarily talk to, and these were places of which I had no experience: industrial places, warehouses; wide open, draughty spaces where bottles of wine and beer were passed from bins filled with ice. There were smoky little bars, members' rooms and pool halls. It was another city; a city that belonged to you.

These friends of yours talked like peacocks, their vocabulary and arguments showy and bright. If they discussed television it was in a way I did not recognize, and if they mentioned a book or a film or an art work, I had invariably never heard of it. As a group they were unsettling company. I never really knew what they thought of me, of my quiet presence on the edge of the group. I found that the best way to assimilate was to listen to the eddying conversation and give dry, ironic answers when asked direct questions. You were proud when I did that; I could see it behind your thick-rimmed spectacles.

○

You liked to test me. You were mischievous that way. One night we met up with Mary and the two of you took me to a fetish club. Your faces glowed as you explained what I would see. I said it sounded fun, and you looked at me oddly.

'We don't have to go, you know,' you whispered as we walked. 'I just thought it would be interesting.'

'It certainly sounds that,' I said.

The fact was that the rubber, the harnesses, the corsetry, the dead-eyed looks from the costumed patrons no longer seemed frightening. Besides, it was hot and underwhelming at the club. So very dark we could barely see the leather and chaps. Mary went off almost immediately, kissing us both on the cheek before disappearing. A woman walked past with a man on a leash. He drank from a bowl of water on the floor. We headed to the bar, not talking. I didn't want to embarrass myself, or make the wrong impression.

'Are you into this?' you said. 'Does it turn you on?'

'It's interesting,' I said pointing to a man with something resembling a long, tasselled tail inserted into his rectum. 'But I can't say it does much for me.'

'Spoilsport,' you said. You smiled but I didn't know whether you were joking. We watched Mary beat the hell out of some guy, then went back to your flat.

○

You never liked staying at my house. It was my great aunt's old place, a three-bedroomed semi with bay windows and a postage stamp garden. I had tried to spruce it up, but I understood your lack of enthusiasm.

'This place has death in it,' you said. 'And not in a good way. I mean, it doesn't give it character. This place *has* no character, this place has no soul. You could refit the whole place and you'd still feel an old woman's last breaths on the back of your shoulders.'

In that first year you spent the night no more than five times. I preferred the brown walls of your high-rise flat anyway, the battered sofas and the old bed that creaked whenever we moved. The lift always smelled of piss and metal – nostalgic, like the stink of old telephone boxes – and I remained as in love with the view from the lounge as ever: it made me feel like I was part of a living, breathing organism. It made me feel alive.

After a year or so, I sold the house and together we bought an apartment on the top floor of a former mental institution in Dalston. The agent told us that John Merrick, the Elephant Man, had been an inmate for a time, and you loved that story almost as much as the exposed brickwork and pitch-pine floors. From the bedroom windows you could see Victoria Park in one direction and all the way down to Liverpool Street in the other. On the night we moved in, the two of us looked out of the second bedroom and toasted it with a bottle of Cava. You put your hand on the window and leaned your head against the pane.

'I can do work here,' you said. 'Real work.'

○

You set up your studio in the spare room and spent all your days in there, the stereo turned up so loud our neighbours complained to the environmental health. When I got back from work you would come out from the studio and have a shower. I would pour some wine and strip out of my work suit. We were still living out of boxes months after moving in and the teetering stacks taunted me, but I couldn't bring myself to unpack everything. I kept telling myself I'd do it on the weekend, or one night the following week, but it never happened; just like quitting smoking, joining the gym and the nights without drinking.

You might disagree, but I think that was when you were actually at your happiest. Fresh from the water, a towel around your body, a glass of wine in your hand, a cigarette burning. You would sit on the toilet seat and tell me about your day and I would listen; then, like a watery town crier, I'd tell you what I'd read in the newspapers. When we were ready, we'd take a cab to wherever we were going next. You never thought of the money: you just liked the feel of a taxi ride through the city streets.

I thought of money, though. I thought about the debts we were accruing, the way we were spending our income. I had always been frugal, but just eighteen months of our being together had begun to burn through my savings and other investments. You'd had small jobs here and there, part-time things, freelance things, but nothing concrete. It frustrated me, but I knew there was no point in my saying anything. So when you were offered that job, I was delighted. It was a good position, a creative role, and one that was handsomely paid. You were wearing jogging bottoms and a vest top when you told me all about it. You did not smile once.

I was confused; then angry. You were proposing to turn it down. You gave me excuses and called them reasons. It would interfere with your real work; it was too far from home; you would be cooped up on a train for two or more hours a day. When you started talking about a new project, one that you were sure would be a success, I lost my temper.

'Can't you just for once in your life think of us and not just of yourself? Of what might be good for us?'

'You don't get it, do you?' you said. 'What's good for me *is* good for us. Do you really want me to be a wage slave? A suit and a bouncy haircut? All teeth and tits? Can you honestly see me like that? This is me, I can't change it and I make no fucking apology for it either. You want me to take the job? You want me to be a commercial artist? I mean, do you even know what being a commercial artist means?' you said. You paused and lit a cigarette.

'But maybe that's what you want,' you went on. 'What you've always wanted. A house, a job, maybe some cute kids, then out to the suburbs and the *Daily Mail*? Is that what this is all about, Ben? You want me to fuck all my ambitions? You want me to be like you; clinging with whitened knuckles to other people's talent?'

The wine glass missed you by several inches and I left you to pick up the shards.

○

There was a game on in the Faltering Fullback, Fulham *v* Bolton. Tom and I sat to the left-hand side of the big screen. I'd said as much as I could and he'd listened as well as he was able, and now we were watching the second half.

'You want to stay at mine tonight?' Tom said.

'I don't know,' I said. 'I should go back really. Don't want her thinking I've just popped out for cigarettes.'

We both smiled. It was an in-joke from our first years in London. Back then, Tom and I shared a one-bedroomed flat above a twenty-four-hour video shop. We both worked nights at a data entry place in Hornsey and would come home after a shift, rent a couple of videos and watch them while playing elaborate drinking games. We loved dumb action pictures, cop dramas, who-dunnits; films that were formulaic, derivative and wonderfully predictable. And it was the clichés we loved: the black best friend shot in the opening moments, the man who disappears after popping out for cigarettes, the cop on the edge, the boss taking him off the case, the trustworthy mentor turning out to be the bad guy. We lived like that for almost six months, in a state of boozy camaraderie. It was the only part of my past that you thought was kind of cool.

You called just as the final whistle was about to blow. Tom made his excuses and went to the bar. I picked up the phone and held it close to my ear without answering it. When I eventually did, I listened to the sound of your breathing.

'You don't understand,' you said. 'I don't mean to be like this. Will you come home, now, please? Will you?'

'I'm sorry,' I said. 'I shouldn't have lost it like that.'

'So you'll come home?'

'I'll be home as soon as I can.'

I said goodbye to Tom and got a cab back to the flat.

○

You turned down the job anyway. Not that you told me straight away. By then it didn't matter; you'd finally sold one of your pieces. You were showing with a bunch of other people at a space in Bethnal Green and there was a lot of interest. It was a new thing for you, an installation: hats on wires. A whole room full of them, caps and homburgs and boaters and bowlers, and everyone loved it. I was late to the opening. By the time I arrived you had already sold it to a collector and were talking to him and a group that he had brought along. You introduced me to James, Johnny, Jimmy, Davey, Mickey, Jane and Iola as your partner and manager. They all said how much they loved the hats.

You seemed slightly nervous around them, but grew steadily calmer. We moved from the gallery to another bar and then got a cab to another one. My head was spinning from the drink and the effort. We left the club and under the dulled lights of Brick Lane spent some time looking for a place that Mickey knew. We eventually ended up in the back room of a Turkish snooker hall, drinking warm bottles of Efes and smoking foreign cigarettes. James, Johnny, Jimmy, Davey, Mickey, Jane and Iola were doing drugs, smoking them off foil. And then I watched as you did the same. In the bathroom there was a long, coiled turd in the toilet bowl. I vomited over it and flushed the stinking mess away.

I was supposed to be in work the next day. I left a message for my boss claiming violent stomach cramps. It was the first time I had ever called in sick.

○

Things changed then. We were sucked – willingly perhaps – into a darker orbit of which I was desperately unsure. I did not like the drugs, nor the effect that they had on you and James, Johnny, Jimmy, Davey, Mickey, Jane and Iola. This new crowd, these new people, were moneyed and classless. They took to you immediately, and placed you at the heart of their little group. Unlike your other friends, they saw no need for me. The odd dry comment was insufficient. They were too dry themselves. They eyed me with superstition, like I was a spy in their ranks.

You would not have a word said against them, though. These people. This group who hunted the darkening streets looking for something, anything, to give them the slightest bristle of excitement. They said they admired Michael Alig, a club promoter who had killed his lover and cut him up into pieces. There was no trace of irony when they mentioned his name.

You called them a support network; you called them friends. And it was hard not to see the effect that they had on you. You were being taken seriously, you were being listened to and considered. When you were with them you were, though it hurts me to say this, incandescent. I have never seen such beauty, such conviction, such passion in anyone. But that was tempered by a newly found cynicism. You began to talk differently: harder, more direct. You saw the illness in people more, you looked for their dark places. At night, in bed, when you were drunk or stoned, you asked me to bind you, to strike you just to see what it would feel like. One evening you asked me to put a cigarette out on your arm. I didn't want to do it, but you insisted. I thought the smell would never leave me.

We were invited to so many parties and openings. These people. This James, Johnny, Jimmy, Davey, Mickey, Jane and Iola. They probably didn't expect me always to be there, but I couldn't trust them to have you all to themselves. You never complained about my presence, not to me at least.

Davey used to call me Minder. I disliked and distrusted him the most.

You expected me to keep you informed of when and where we were supposed to be going. I bought you an electronic gizmo to help you get organized, but you destroyed it and made it part of one of your works. I only discovered this when I saw its metal insides and wires glued to a piece of parquet flooring. You thanked me with kisses for the inspiration. It was the second piece you sold.

○

After that you sold two more pieces. One for a relatively large amount of money. It was a portrait of the building in which we lived, but inside each of the windows there was a tiny crime scene; a dead body, blood spatter, a murder weapon. James, Johnny, Jimmy, Davey, Mickey, Jane and Iola said that it marked the beginning of a new phase for you. They said you were big time; that you had a rare understanding of society and art. At home your work was taking over the communal areas: there were paint splashes on the walls, flecks on the floorboards.

I suggested that with the money we take a holiday, get away from the sweat and temper of the city for a while.

'Are you fucking *crazy?*' you said. 'I've just sold four pieces, I've got to keep going, keep the momentum up. Look, you go if you want, please go. But I've got work I've got to do here, okay?'

'It's just for a week, love,' I said. 'Just seven days.'

'I don't have seven days,' you said. 'I've got to keep working.'

○

I flew out to Cyprus the following week accompanied by Tom. He was surprised by my offer – we'd not seen each other for a good few months – but seemed to appreciate it. You gave me a thoughtless, distracted goodbye and suddenly I was cut adrift, on my own once again.

Tom had shaved off his beard and was wearing shorts and flip-flops. He already looked relaxed, his well-padded frame wedged into a metal chair. We were drinking Guinness in the airport bar and he was talking about an old school friend – Rebecca Johns – whom he'd recently met. Apparently she'd got divorced and was now living with a fifty-year-old lawyer and his two children. Tom began reminiscing about the time Rebecca and the two of us had gone to get tattoos. We'd all chickened out.

'I've got a tattoo now,' I said.

Tom paused. 'A tattoo? Really? Where?'

I took off my jacket, hitched up the arm of my T-shirt and showed him the green-black symbol at the top of my bicep.

'When did you get that?'

'Six months ago.'

'Did it hurt?'

'Wrecked. Cara got one at the same time. She was fine though.'

'What did she have?'

'Same thing.'

He shook his head and laughed. He took off his glasses and wiped them on his T-shirt.

'What's funny?' I said. 'I like it.'

Tom looked across the table. The place was lit unforgivingly by the large window. The drone from the airfield gave the room a humming kind of tension. Tom picked up his drink.

'Here's to holidays,' he said with a smile that exposed the fat wriggle of his tongue.

O

I wrote on the postcard *you would love it here*, but knew that you wouldn't. The light was sometimes unbearable: the sun insistent, the sea star-tipped and roiling green. We went down to the beach every day. I lay under a parasol and read cheap thrillers, leaving the difficult novels and biographies back at the hotel. Tom spent most of the day asleep beside me, toasting his flesh a salmon pink. We played football when the tide was out and others joined in. I swam in the sea, the water as clear as gin.

In the evenings we would eat at a beachside restaurant then head for the bars. Most nights there was live football and we played a lot of cards. We did not talk about art or books or culture or politics. We talked about the old days, about films we liked, quoted lines from television shows we used to love. We discussed football tactics and made up impossible quizzes. We did not talk about you. We never talked about you. Tom would change the subject whenever your name was mentioned.

○

We took a trip to the Troodos mountains. There was snow on the peaks even at that time of year, and the views were humbling. We stopped at a monastery and Tom and I did not talk. For several moments I thought about becoming a monk. I'm sure every man there was thinking the same thing. Simple brown robes, a pair of sandals and that deep, longing silence. The smell of wax candles and incense, the taste of home-made wine, the warm sound of a tolling bell. I watched a line of them shuffle across the courtyard, their bent heads exposing their pale white tonsures. Tom took a photograph. It felt like stealing.

During lunch both Tom and I were quiet. The restaurant looked out over the mountain range, scrubby brown grasses, verdant trees and the occasional farmhouse. The kleftiko was tender and the wine dry and cold. Two women sat down at the next table. They were fair-haired and curvaceous, Irish-looking. Tom asked them what they thought of the monastery. They paused for a moment as if selecting the minimum amount of words necessary.

'It was very calming,' the woman to my left said. Her accent had a hint of Lancashire; her name was Emma. Tom smiled.

'I was tempted to join the brothers,' he said. 'But I hear it's habit forming.'

They laughed at the weakness of the joke and joined us. I found myself flirting. I thought of this Emma in my bed, her large breasts, her throaty laugh, her appealing spray of freckles. And then I thought of you.

○

As soon as we got back to the villa, I called you. You sounded wired; wired but pleased to hear from me.

'What's it like there? Is it hot?'

'It's hot, yes,' I replied, 'but there's a breeze. It's beautiful actually. We're right by the sea.' I could not recall whether I'd already told you this.

'I've had a great idea. For a piece. I started today.'

'That's good.'

'When are you back?'

'Saturday morning.'

There was a pause, like you were working something out.

'Okay. I'll see you then. I love you.'

'I love you too.'

'Oh and Ben?'

'Yes?'

'I miss you. I miss you so much.'

'I miss you too,' I said.

○

That night Tom and Maria slept together. They left Emma and me on the balcony, drinking wine and making small talk. We almost kissed. It was harder not to than you can imagine. She had just broken up with her husband, a telemarketer from Oldham, and the emotion of it was still raw. There were no tears as she told me about it, about the dull predictability of a dull relationship. I told her about you, about how the one thing you never were was dull.

'It must be hard for you, though,' Emma said. 'Putting up with all that.'

'With what?'

'You know. The tantrums and that. The constant attention. It'd wear me out. It were bad enough with Gary and his moods. But give him a beer and a blowie and he were fine. Well. At least I thought he was. The way you talk about Cara, she sounds . . . you know. Difficult.'

I picked up the cigarettes and weighed them in my hand.

'She means everything to me,' I said. 'I honestly can't bear the thought of being without her.'

'That's the way I used to feel about cigarettes,' Emma said, laughing. 'Now I can't stand the sight of them.'

She talked some more about Gary and we finished the wine. When she went to bed, I lay on the living-room sofa with an aching erection. I was trying to think of you.

○

You did not pick me up from the airport. London was rain-lashed and metal grey. Tom and I took the Tube across the city, the carriage a mix of those excited to be in the capital and those dismayed at their return. We both fell asleep quickly and were lucky not to miss our stop. There was sand in my socks and the smell of suntan lotion on my skin.

'Thanks for a great time,' I said as we said goodbye at King's Cross.

'Keep in touch,' Tom said. 'Don't leave it months like last time. I could be married by then.'

I slammed the door of his taxi and walked to the bus stop. I waited for a while and when the bus came I suddenly felt nauseous. I rode it out until Essex Road and then had to get off. The pubs had just opened and I headed into the Duke of Marlborough. It was dark, the lights not yet lit, the only illumination the green wash from a television screen showing the racing. I ordered red wine and sat down on a sofa and pulled out one of the books I had intended to read on the beach. Then you rang. You called me to ask how I was getting on. You sounded excited. I was about to say that there had been a delay and I'd be home in an hour or so, but then I heard your voice properly, its tender spell. I finished my drink and hurried out into the filthy city rain.

○

You were wearing a short skirt and a T-shirt when I got back. You kissed me passionately and we talked for a little while before you pulled me into the bedroom. I wanted to last longer, but I'd forgotten the softness of your skin, the way your body felt when against mine. Afterwards we shared a cigarette, your cheek on my chest and

I looked around at the mess you had left. There were plates and pizza boxes on the floor, empty bottles of wine and full ashtrays. Later I would tidy them away, I thought, after I'd put the washing on and had a shower. You kissed my nipple and then sneezed. You ran your fingers through my chest hair and pulled at it slightly, as though checking it was still attached.

'Things are going to be so much better,' you said. 'I can feel it.'

She finished the last of the cigarette and then yawned.

'I finished that project, by the way,' you said. 'The one I told you about. I gave it to Johnny on Wednesday and he just can't stop going on about it. Says it's the best thing he's seen in years. I mean, he was raving about it. You know what he's usually like, right? All tight-lipped and dour? He's practically coming in his pants watching it.'

'That's great. Wonderful news. What kind of thing is it?'

'Film. Well, it's sort of a montage . . . It's hard to explain, but I think it's the best thing I've ever done, Ben. That's what Johnny says anyway. The best thing I've ever done.'

'What's it about?' I said, looking again to the dirty floor.

'Sex and death,' you said and laughed. 'What else?'

You refused to say any more about it. Apparently Johnny thought that the power of the piece came from its surprise, and you didn't want to spoil it for me.

'But the papers are interested,' you said. 'Johnny even thinks we might get some television.'

'Honey, Johnny's full of shit most of the time.'

'Everyone's full of shit,' you said. 'Surely you know that by now?'

○

We'd been to Johnny's gallery several times before, but there was something different about it when we arrived: there was expectation. You were being profiled for *Frieze* and this meant something to all of them. You made it: they all made it. James, Johnny, Jimmy, Davey, Mickey, Jane and Iola. There was music playing in the background, something discordant on a cello. We drank bottles of Beck's and glasses of wine, and watched as the space filled up. They looked at each face, con-

ferred with each other about its relative importance. I watched them all, so many people; more
than I had ever seen at any of these things before.

James, Johnny, Jimmy, Davey, Mickey, Jane,
Iola and I were outside. We were smoking cigarettes and I was listening to them talk about how
you were effectively rewriting what was expected
of modern female artists. A couple – a pair of
vastly more successful artists who were now working with rock bands on their promotional videos –
came over to join us. I was introduced and they
shot me a familiar smile, one that acknowledged a
non-combatant.

Then you were there. You were dressed in a
black halter top and a short black skirt. Your nails
were polished and your lipstick red.

'Today is made for the vamp,' you'd said as you
were dressing, 'the ingénue must stay at home.'

I handed you a drink. You did not look unset-
tled, rather you looked complete.

'Aren't you nervous?' I said as we walked inside, through the crowd and up to the dais.

'A little, but the journalist? She loved it. She's
saying it's a defining work.'

I looked around at the collecting group and

thought that they all looked the same, all dressed in black and charcoal grey. I got another drink and waited as Johnny introduced you.

○

Johnny finished his gushing praise and you took your place behind the microphone. They were applauding you without having seen the film. Then the clapping stopped and you began to speak. This is what you said:

*Thank you all very much for coming. I didn't really think I had so many friends and family. This is a special piece for me, one that I've been thinking about for several years but which has only recently managed to come together. It has a rather long and abstract title, but then I've always had fun with words. It is dedicated with love to my partner, Ben, who was good enough to leave the country for a week while I finished it.*

This is what we all saw projected onto the back wall of the gallery. What you made. Your art work: *Artistic and Naturalistic Representations of Sex and Death in its Concurrent States.*

At first the screen is black. Then the audio track begins. *Oh yes! Oh fuck! Oh yes!* There is a man. He is naked. He is in a room with pale wooden floors. A blonde woman is on her knees. She is sucking his penis. Behind them there are two women sitting on a sofa. They are naked. They are kissing. One has dark hair, the other has blonde hair. The woman with blonde hair is otherwise hairless. The man is watching the two women. The two women stop kissing. Then the dark-haired woman begins to lick the hairless woman's vagina. The man keeps watching. The woman on her knees continues to suck his penis.

The screen goes blank for a moment. Then there is footage of a news report. It is the middle of a bulletin. The presenter is in a studio and he is American. He has white teeth and an orange cast to his skin. He says: ... *shooting in Malibu late Wednesday night. It is the fifth such gang-related incident to have occurred in the last week. Here's Shola Singh with more.* The scene shifts to the streets of Malibu. Shola Singh has hair that resembles a crash helmet. She looks intently at the camera and says: *Homicide detectives were called to the residence at 3.17 a.m. this morning* ...

The sound then lowers and is replaced by pornographic moaning.

The screen cleaves in two. On the left-hand side, the three women are now taking it in turns to suck the man's penis. On the right-hand side the report into the shooting continues.

*[left]* He puts his penis in the blonde woman's mouth.

*[right]* There is a picture of the victim. His name is Diego Riera, 23. He was shot 16 times. A detective appeals for witnesses. We go back to the studio.

*[left]* He puts his penis in the anus of the dark-haired woman.

*[right]* 'In Oakland,' the anchorman says, 'the funeral of pornographic actor Mark Steele caused controversy today. Demonstrators from the families of Jayne Lou Michaels, known as Jayne Raine, Michelle de La Hoya, known as Jenna Levein and Angela Griffin, known as Angel Lord, disrupted this morning's small service. Here's Tammy Fallon at The Shepherd's Bay Funeral Parlour.

*[left]* The blonde woman sucks the man's penis the moment it comes out of the dark-haired

woman's anus. He puts his penis in the anus of the other blonde woman.

*[right]* Tammy Fallon has bleached blonde hair and is wearing a purple dress. She pauses then speaks, 'The families were angered by the court's decision that no civil reparations will be lodged against Steele's estate. This follows allegations that Steele deliberately faked a mandatory HIV test prior to the shooting of the pornographic film *The Lost Girls*. All performers later tested positive for HIV. Michaels, de La Hoya, and Griffin all died last year.'

*[left]* He puts his penis in the dark-haired woman's mouth. He puts his penis in the vagina of the dark-haired woman.

*[right]* 'They were killed by that man,' a woman says. She is the mother of the other blonde woman. They show a photograph of the dead man. Then a picture of the other blonde woman. 'He as good as put a gun to their head and pulled the trigger.'

*[left]* He takes his penis in his hand. The three women line up in front of him.

*[right]* 'He can't pay for his crime, but we demand justice,' a man says. He is the father of

the dark-haired woman. They show a picture of the dark-haired woman, then a photograph of the blonde woman. Tammy Fallon looks serious.

*[left]* The man ejaculates over their faces. The three women kiss.

*[right]* Then the reporter says: 'Tammy Fallon, CBS news, Oakland.'

The screens fade to black.

○

For a moment there was silence. Then the applause came. James, Johnny, Jimmy, Davey, Mickey, Jane and Iola looked almost tearful. As one, the crowd turned to you in congratulation. As I was brushed aside by well-wishers, I overheard someone say: 'Sex and death. So simple, yet so . . . expressive.' Another voice: 'The use of split screen, such duality, was inspired.' And another: 'It says all it needs to say about our obsession with masculinity.' And another: 'The artistic eye is uncanny. It's naked; both beautiful and ugly.' And another: 'This is one of those moments, you know? A real where-were-you? moment.'

And the applause and the talk overwhelmed me. I went and got myself a drink and sat down. I watched you talk, take the adulation. You glowed in the reflection of their praise, your painted face ghostly under the lamps. I hardly recognized you at all.

○

After half an hour, you came over and put your arm around me.

'Sorry, honey, it's been crazy. Everyone loves it. Just loves it! What do you think? You love it too?'

I looked down at my drink. 'I thought it was simple yet expressive,' I said. 'That the split screen was inspired. That it was both beautiful and ugly.'

You had a theory that heaven is the constant repetition of the happiest moment of your life.

'Are you okay?' you said.

'I'm fine,' I said. 'Go talk to your public.'

'You sure?'

'Positive,' I said. You kissed me on the cheek.

I picked up my jacket. 'I'll see you later,' I said.

'You're not going, are you? You can't go yet,' you said. 'There's loads of people you need to meet.'

'I'll see them later,' I said. 'I'm just popping out for cigarettes.'

# Sometimes Nothing,
# Sometimes Everything

My possessions did not take up much space in the removals van. Six boxes, a suitcase, and a standard lamp I didn't even like. Mark had a lot of stuff. A cactus, a sofa, a hostess trolley; a huge oak chest of drawers. Somewhere amongst these items a clock was ticking. I wondered what kind of clock could tick that loudly and resolved to remove its batteries as soon as we arrived at our new home.

After the van was fully loaded, I sat on the motorized loading bay and pressed the illuminated button. It took me up and down at a steady, even pace. Mark watched me from the pavement, panting, his hands on his hips and sweat marks already visible on his T-shirt. I took my finger off the button mid climb and jumped off the platform.

'Come on, Joe,' he said. 'Can we please just get going?'

I pushed open the gate and walked through the front door. The flat looked distressed and naked without Andrea's things; like a clown without make-up. I walked down the hallway where there should have been a Portuguese *Vertigo* poster and a signed photograph of Sophia Loren. In the lounge where the large mirror she'd bought at a car boot fair used to hang, there was simply a white space with a nicotine-tinged halo. On the carpet there was a strand of her auburn hair and a collection of stains: red wine, curry, a smudge of lipstick. Could a scientist animate Andrea from what she'd left behind, I wondered? And if so, would she still go and leave me anyway?

I felt an arm on my shoulder. Mark was modern like that and I shrugged him off. I went into the kitchen, a room cleaner than it had been for the whole time we'd lived there. I turned on the tap and then turned it off again for no good reason. Outside the window, a crow had landed on the thin, rusting balcony.

'A crow,' I said. 'Crows? Aren't they bad omens?'

'No,' Mark said and sighed. 'That's ravens, Joe.

Or magpies perhaps. Not crows. Definitely not crows. Now come on, it's time to go.'

I went into what was once our bedroom. It was dark in there and it smelled slightly funky; no longer fragranced by Andrea's perfume or those room deodorizers she always bought. I looked down onto the street. The old man from the corner shop was talking to a woman holding a plant pot. A kid whizzed past on a bike and an old man in a suit and tie paused to tie his shoelace. A youth in sportswear talked loudly on his phone, his dog brushed and brutish alongside him. Andrea used to say she loved this part of town because it was both belligerent and beautiful; beautiful and belligerent, just like her.

I sat down on the bed, remembering the day we'd moved in; those first few moments. In this room, I'd complained bitterly about all Andrea's stuff. 'Surely,' I'd said, my hands full of pillows, 'you don't need all these cushions.' She'd said nothing and instead started unpacking a large cardboard box with 'Hats' written on it in marker pen.

'What's funny?' Mark said.

I looked at the floor and then at the window.

'Sometimes nothing,' I said. 'Sometimes everything.'

○

It poured with rain as Mark drove the van across the city. It was hard to see more than a few feet in front and for a moment I imagined us skidding off the road, down an embankment, dying in agony as the neatly stacked boxes of our possessions were punctured and slashed. Mark leant forward in his seat, the windows steamed, his eyes on the brake lights of the cars in front. We stalled at an intersection and Mark furiously tried to get the van back into gear. A woman walked along the pavement, so wet through now there was no point in her running for shelter. The freezing rain beat down on the cab. I sat staring at the *A-to-Z*, hoping that our new home was nowhere near here.

We pulled up outside a pebble-dashed terrace some moments later. There was a front garden slick with leaves and litter, three windows with drawn curtains, an aluminium front door. It had a kind of horrific normality, as though beyond its anonymous facade bodies were buried or child pornography was filmed. I thought about sounding the horn to give Mark a scare — he was always jumpy — but thought better of it.

O

My new bedroom looked out over the street. The walls were a sort of claret colour, the flooring dark wooden boards, slightly bowed as if they had come from a galleon. On the west wall two enormous wardrobes dwarfed my clothes and under the window there was an old scarred table with a brass desk lamp and a pub-stolen ashtray set on it. I hung a picture on the free wall, an advert for Michelin tyres I'd had for years, and put the final unpacked box in the wardrobe.

I didn't leave the house for two weeks. Mark got me what I needed and didn't ask too many questions. Mostly I was working, lines of code spewing from my fingers, but sometimes I was thinking. I spent a lot of time listening to foreign radio stations, country stations, classical stations, any kind of radio that didn't remind me of her. My favourite was an American oldies station, not for the songs so much as the adverts: the car dealership offers, the swap meets, the impenetrable politicking on clauses 7, 11 and 14.

When he was in and lonely, Mark would sit on my bed with a beer or a glass of wine and tell me about his day. I would grunt and nod, play Minesweeper or maybe go back to the coding. He wanted me to talk to him honestly about how I was feeling; he didn't think it was healthy to be in the house all the time, fogging up the bedroom with ash and cigarette smoke. I would neither agree nor disagree with him, and after a while he'd give up and go downstairs to watch the television or something. He always asked if I wanted to join him, and one evening I surprised myself, genuinely, by accepting.

○

'The most difficult thing is realizing you're on your own. Don't you think?'

'I like being on my own,' I said. 'It's an important part of who I am.'

'I'm walking down the road sometimes and it just hits me. If I don't come home tonight, who's going to care? Who's going to notice, you know? Or call? And that's scary. That's really scary.' Mark was wearing shorts and a T-shirt because the heating was up so high. He had been trying to get me to talk since the football had kicked off.

'Plenty of people are alone,' I said. 'Being alone is the default position for most people. The whole notion of us being social animals, social beings, is just rubbish.'

He shook his head. 'You do talk some shit, Joe.'

I lit a cigarette and drank the last of my wine. 'You listen to it,' I said. 'So what does that make you?'

He ignored me and wiped the back of his hand across his mouth.

'You been out this week?'

'Nope.'

'I don't know how you stand it, cooped up in here day after day.'

'It soothes me.'

'You're like a child,' he said.

'Yeah, the child you never had, right?'

Mark got up and left the room. I heard his door close and his stereo click on. I finished my cigarette. My mouth felt like the baize on a pool table. I picked up my wallet from the top of the mantel and turned off the television. By the front door, I rifled through the jackets, found a set of keys and headed outside.

○

The night-time air had a rushing quality, and the trees that lined the street were blown by its gusts. There were puddles in the pits of the road and the low orange light from the street lamps shone on a birdshit-caked Astra with an instruction to move pasted to its windscreen. I walked left then right and made it to the main road. A car flashed past, a colossal beat coming from the bass cone of its speakers. A group of smokers was hanging around outside a Kurdish social club, their cigarettes poking their moustaches like slim fingers.

I followed the road down, past the fried chicken place, the kebab house and another chicken shop until I came to an off-licence. The attendant was talking quickly into his mobile, a bottle of Supermalt open in front of him. I walked down the aisles and wondered what would be a suitable gift to appease Mark. In amongst the cheap red wine I saw a bottle of Chianti wrapped in a fancy sackcloth covering, and decided on that.

'It's nice that one,' the man said as I passed it to him. 'Looks nice too.'

I gave him a twenty and nodded.

'Thank you,' he said handing me the change. 'Goodbye now.'

Taking the coins, I felt like I had accomplished something. The shopkeeper had been friendly throughout; in fact more than friendly, he had been warm. A couple walked towards me arm in arm and I noticed the man almost imperceptibly incline his head towards me as I passed them. A bus drove by, then a squad car. For some reason both were reassuring.

○

When I got back inside, the heat hit me like a gloved punch. I went upstairs and knocked on Mark's door. He was sitting in an armchair with his phone in his hand. He did this a lot, staring at the phone, wondering whether she would ever call him and too scared to ring her himself. Mark looked up; I could tell he'd been crying and I hoped it wasn't because of what I'd said.

'Peace offering,' I said. 'I even went outside to buy it. It's Chianti.'

Mark gave me a sad little sigh and got up. He took the bottle and placed it on the window-sill.

'You can put a candle in it when you've drunk it,' I said.

'Thanks,' Mark said. 'I'll bear that in mind.'

'Friends?' I said.

He nodded and ushered me out of the room. I heard him change the music, the soft voice of a hushed man. I went into my room and smoked a couple of cigarettes and decided what to do with the following day.

○

I woke early and had a shower, put on some washing then surveyed what was in my cupboards. I made a list of items I needed and then checked online for the nearest supermarket. It seemed there was one in a shopping complex some half mile away. I walked there, the huge Asda sign a green beacon in the distance. As I approached, it looked like it was floating, unattached. I stopped at the edge of the car park and wished I had a camera with me; it was the kind of photo I'd like to look at. I put my fingers into a square and framed the shot. It was beautiful.

There was a small parade of boarded-up shops and in front of them a man had set up a cup-and-ball game on a fold-out picnic table. He was conning a crowd of muscled Poles out of money to send home, and they seemed happy to be handing over the cash. Further along there were more hawkers selling pirated DVDs, Spanish razor blades, counterfeit underwear and blister packs of Duracell batteries. By the time I got to the door of the Asda I had ignored seventeen separate opportunities to purchase dodgy goods of all kinds.

In the cavernous Asda I fumbled over the crème caramels in the dairy section: they were Andrea's favourites and we always kept some in the fridge, just in case. I held them in my hand for a little while, the cold air from the refrigerator numbing my arm, until eventually I put them down. I didn't even like crème caramels.

My trolley was half full when I pranged it on someone else's. The man looked at me with sympathetic eyes and apologized.

'Oh no,' I said, 'it was my fault, I wasn't looking where the hell I was going.'

He had a beard and sidelocks and gentle features. He was the first Hasid I'd ever seen and it made me happy to be out of the house and meeting new people. I nodded and made my way to the checkouts.

None of the queues were too long, but I was a little unsure as to which one to join. In the end I decided upon aisle five, which was staffed by a blond-haired man. He had psoriasis on his left hand and he scratched at it in between scanning items. When it was my turn, he looked up from his cash register. 'Would you like help packing?' he asked in a voice that suggested he would immediately walk out of the shop if I said yes.

His nametag said Eamon and I couldn't fathom how he had become stuck bagging shopping and scanning goods when he clearly had something more to offer the world. At that moment, I would have done anything to help him. Anything at all. I imagined him eating his evening meals in one of those builders' cafes, a paper open as he chewed shepherd's pie with three vegetables, and the sadness almost overtook me. This man – what, my age? younger? – hearing the bleeps, the constant bleeps of the products, hearing them like an echocardiogram counting out his remaining heartbeats.

Eamon smiled as he handed me my till receipt. He wished me a good day, and I wished him the same. I meant it, too.

○

I walked the other way around the mall and passed more street vendors. I wasn't tempted by anything until I saw two women standing between Currys and Sports Direct. They were holding out packets of rolling tobacco, Marlboro Lights, Benson & Hedges and Silk Cut.

'How much for Marlboros?' I said. The blonde woman named her price in a deep Eastern European accent; it was well under half what I paid at the supermarket. Her eyes were grey and her cheekbones made her look like one of those vacant, ice-queen models who never appears to enjoy life. But when she smiled, this woman looked like she had invented the very idea of happiness.

'How many you like?'

'A carton,' I said and her big grey eyes got bigger. She unshouldered her rucksack and took out the cigarettes. The health warning on them was in Cyrillic. I thanked her and asked if she was often here. She looked at me slightly funny.

'You police?'

'Do I look like police?'

'No. You look like . . . you know, skateboarder.'

'So are you here all the time?' I said. She nodded.

'Good,' I said, 'I'll make sure I only buy cigarettes from you. My name is Joe, by the way.'

'Coco,' she said. 'Everyone calls me Coco.'

'Like the clown?' I said.

'No, like Chanel,' she said.

○

It was the beginning of a routine. Every Thursday I would walk past the hawkers and the DVD vendors to do my weekly shop. I'd get in line and Eamon would offer a faint smile of recognition and I would wish him a good day and mean it. I'd then wander round to Coco and exchange a brief few words with her and her silent accomplice. She'd pass me my carton of Marlboros and say, 'See you soon.' The best part of the week was always the smile she gave me as I left. That would keep my cheeks burning all the way home.

After the initial tension, living with Mark became much easier. The two of us fell into a familiar and comforting kind of life. I would cook on weeknights and Mark on the weekends. We shared washing duties and he paid for all the channels on the television. We sometimes played chess, sometimes went to the pub or met up with other friends in town. It was the right, correct thing to do and I felt something had altered, that a ship had been steadied. I still thought of Andrea, but the hurt wasn't quite as livid as before.

○

The fifth time I bought cigarettes from Coco was a bitter day and she was wearing a beanie hat; her nose red-tipped from the cold. As I walked away, I thought about her chilled to the bone and bought her a large coffee from Subway. She thanked me in a cautious way, then gave me that smile. She took the paper cup and as she did our hands briefly brushed against each other. I made my way home in a daze, delighting in the crackle between our fingers.

Over the weeks my mood changed and I became more spritely at home, more conversational. I didn't talk about Coco, though; not to Mark, not to anyone. Mark wouldn't have understood anyway. He had already given me a considerable lecture on the moral ambiguities of buying illegal cigarettes. I'd just told him there was nothing ambiguous about the price. Mark shook his head at this and hadn't mentioned it again – save for an occasional whispered comment.

Coco and I began to linger over our transactions, to exchange little nuggets of personal information. She lived about a mile and a half away in a shared house with nine other women. I found that out on week six. That she had two sisters back in the Ukraine, that was week seven. Week nine she told me that she didn't like much Western music, but she didn't mind Coldplay. Week eleven, I gave her a CD of the music I liked and said that not all Western music was Coldplay.

Week twelve she told me she liked some of the songs, but that some were too loud. She told me on week fifteen that she had trouble sleeping because her room-mate – Lenka, the woman who stood by her side as we talked – snored like a rattling train. She also told me that she had recently started smoking again and wished that she hadn't.

I told her about Andrea on week nineteen, and she said that she felt sorry for me. She told me that her husband had gone missing a long time ago and that she'd almost forgotten what he looked like. Week twenty-one, I told her that I secretly called my home The House of Abandoned Men and she laughed at that and said she couldn't imagine such a place. She had a cold on week twenty-four and so I bought her some soup and told her to go home. She said I was kind.

On week twenty-five I told her that I'd found this great new cafe bar. It had recently opened and they did the best pasta sauce I'd ever tasted – she'd revealed her favourite foods, along with her dislikes (cucumbers, cauliflower) on week seventeen. She said the cafe sounded nice, but I couldn't quite bring myself to ask her to join me. Week twenty-seven I almost invited her but instead told her that we had a mouse in our kitchen. Coco said that if they had a mouse at her house, it would probably fall into Lenka's open, snoring mouth.

○

On week thirty I said goodbye to Eamon and wished him a good day, but I didn't mean it quite as much as usual. The thing between Coco and me had become somewhat tortuous. I wanted there to be no transactions, no moral ambiguity. I wanted it to be just the two of us, lost and lonely, sharing a coffee or a meal of some kind. But every time I came close to asking, I thought of Andrea, her face cold and impassive like the rocks you get at springs.

'Oh holy living Christ, Joe,' she'd said, 'I can't do this any more. Not one more day. I'm leaving, and I'm leaving now before I end up killing you.'

Two more weeks went by, and the flick-flack image of Andrea wouldn't leave me. I thought I'd changed, but how can you really tell? Then I saw the new Coldplay record in the supermarket and knew just what to do. I bought it from Eamon along with my other shopping and felt confident that this would be the week. I walked past a man selling knock-off cosmetics and an old homeless guy jangling change in his cupped hands. It felt like they were urging me on from the touchlines.

Between Currys and Sports Direct, Lenka was there as usual but instead of Coco, a dark-haired woman with sad oval eyes was standing beside her. Lenka looked away; the other woman looked at me.

'Cigarette?'

'Where's Coco?' I said.

'Cigarette?'

I turned to Lenka.

'Lenka, where's Coco?'

Lenka looked down.

'Who is Coco? You want cigarette? Good price here.'

'No, no cigarettes!' I turned again to Lenka. 'Where is she? I have something for her.'

Lenka leaned in close to me; she smelled of clove oil.

'Go away, there is no Coco here. No Coco, okay?'

'I have this CD for her,' I said. 'She likes them. It's Coldplay, look.'

Lenka looked at the CD in my hand and made to say something but then a man loomed up behind her. He was bear-like and broad and said something to Lenka in Ukrainian. She reached into her bag and passed him two packets of Camels. As he walked past he gave me a shove, my shopping spilling all over the pavement.

A bottle of orange juice landed near Lenka's feet. She picked it up and put it in my hand.

'She liked you,' she said, quickly in a whisper. Then she turned her back on me and spoke in her native tongue with the new woman, the woman who wasn't Coco. I glanced up at the Asda sign; it looked like it was about to float away again.

I stood there without a single idea what to do

next. In the distance there was the distinctive wail of sirens. Lenka looked at the other woman, then stooped to pick up her rucksack. Wordlessly they made their way towards the exit.

# *The Final Cigarette*

He sits on the balcony of the Raised Star Hotel in Reno, newly married, soon to die, about to smoke his last cigarette. He knows it is his last cigarette, and he hopes the coughing won't spoil it. The sun is rising over the casinos and hotels and he is wearing his dark sunglasses; the aviator shades he wears when he goes fishing. He could have a drink if he wanted, but he doesn't. He could easily steal out of the room and down to a bar, but that would hurt the woman he loves and that's not what he does these days. It's become a kind of joke now, this Good Raymond stuff, but it's true. When people say they can die happy, he almost understands that. He smiles and taps his last cigarette against the packet. No one wants to die with a hangover.

There is a cup of coffee steaming on the table in front of him and he wonders for a moment how many cigarettes and how many cups of coffee he has married in his life. The marriage of cigarettes and coffee. I should have written a story called that, he thinks, and realizes that this is the first time he has thought about work since landing in Reno. He is not looking at others, or observing himself, or his new bride. He is no longer transforming one thing into another. It's a bit like being drunk, he thinks: it lends a sort of pitched clarity to your perspective.

He and Tess were married two days ago at the Heart of Reno Wedding Chapel and he'd felt even more nervous than the first time, back when he was twenty. He'd almost joked with Tess that it'd just be his luck to drop down dead while walking down the aisle. But thankfully he'd kept his mouth shut. They've not talked about the cancer since they got here – they are in Reno, after all, and no one talks about cancer in Reno – and he likes to imagine that he's left it back at home, like a difficult, truculent teenager.

He puts the cigarette to his lips. It feels good in his mouth, firm and right. It is a Chesterfield.

When he was in the store, buying his last packet of cigarettes, he needed to decide which brand his last cigarette would be: it was a decision too important to be left to chance or simply to habit.

The first kind he smoked were Wings. They were the cheap cigarettes his father had smoked. He remembers the first one he sneaked. He was nine years old and the party his parents were giving had just come to an end. He took one from the pack, lit it and liked the way the smoke tasted on his tongue. You know instantly if you're a smoker. A proper smoker. His best friend Harvey always seemed uncomfortable with a cigarette: like it wouldn't quite sit right. But Ray's always looked good smoking. He knows that.

Lucky Strikes were his brand when he was old enough to buy his own. He liked the package and the *It's Toasted!* line on the box. They were filterless and harsh but they were smoother than the Wings and they made him feel older. Like anyone in Yakima needed anything to make themselves feel older. He blew his first smoke ring with a Lucky. He smoked a Lucky after the first time he got laid. Luckies were in his breast pocket when he discovered he was going to be a father a year shy of making it out of his teens.

When he moved to Paradise, California, he smoked Kools for a while. But they made his mouth taste too much like mornings. He went on to Kents, then settled on Marlboros. But this last packet, and this last one from this last packet, is a Chesterfield. It's a Chesterfield because Chesterfields remind him of the first day he really knew he'd kicked the booze. He was talking to Tess, smoking a Chesterfield, and he knew that things were just about getting better: that things finally *were* better.

He coughs a little and feels something chunky in his mouth. He worries that when he spits it out it'll be part of his lungs. The blood he's been expelling for months still frightens him, even though there's nothing now left to fear. He stands and puts the cigarette on the small card table and leans over the balcony. There is no one around, no one on the street. He dribbles the spit slowly from his mouth, just like he used to off the Barrelhead Bridge, and watches it cast like a fishing line. A little of it catches on the stubble of his chin. He wipes it away with the back of his hand and smiles a big goofy smile that makes him feel like he's that fat little kid hanging out on the Barrelhead Bridge again.

Ray sits back down in the motel chair and picks up the cigarette. He sniffs at it and takes the lighter from the breast pocket of his shirt. It is a cheap plastic Bic. He has lost a lot of lighters over the course of his life: countless plastic ones, copper Zippos, an engraved Ronson once. But somehow it seems fitting that he'll use a blue Bic lighter he doesn't even remember buying to light that last smoke. He flicks the wheel and nothing happens. He tries again and still nothing. He laughs and tries once more for luck. The thing is busted, unable to do the one thing that is expected of it. He sets down the cigarette again. There is a book of matches in the bedroom, sitting inside an ashtray. He stands up and goes to get them.

The room is cool, almost pitch-dark through the lenses of his sunglasses. Tess is sound asleep. He palms the matches and looks at her sleeping. He hopes her dreams are pleasant; that she's thinking of baccarat tables and reels of slots aligning. On the dresser is $627 in various denominations of bill. Tess can't stop winning in Reno. She's on a hot streak that just won't go cold, but Ray can't hit a card, can't even buy one. He looks at the money and wonders whether he's ever seen so much just lying around without a purpose. He thinks how much he could have used that money years ago. How much he could have used that luck.

Back outside he stands and looks out over Reno. He thinks again of that old Johnny Cash record. The first time he heard it was in the late sixties. A long-haired girl in a bikini had a transistor radio playing in the next yard. It was California hot and he was drinking a beer. When he heard that famous line about shooting a man in Reno, it made him down his drink and go back inside the house to write. He was urged on by the sound of the prisoners cheering as Johnny sang 'Just to watch him die'; but it was mid afternoon and he'd had too much to drink. The poem he'd written was worthless so he'd thrown it away.

Ray puts the cigarette to his lips. The last cigarette. He sparks the match and holds it in his cupped hands until it catches. He sucks in the smoke and fills his lungs.

○

The fag fell and somehow managed to get itself below Dad's dressing gown and half inside his pyjama bottoms. He wriggled in the wheelchair, his arms flailing as he tried to get at it. I paused for a moment, wondering whether or not to help him. Eventually I relented and retrieved the cigarette, putting it in his hand. The smell that clung to his clothes and to his skin was strong, like bad breath. I hoped that the powerful odour would overwhelm the tobacco, and none of the nurses or doctors would look at me with disgust as I wheeled him back to the ward.

The staff had been good to my father, all things considered, and he probably pestered them to help him long before he asked me. But, professionally, I don't think they could be seen to be wheeling a man through the hospital grounds just for the purposes of smoking a fag. Even those who smoked would have seen that it was dubious to grant this dying man his last wish. I've always been more of a pushover.

We were standing, illuminated by low yellow street lamps, at the hospital perimeter. To our right were a couple of nurses, smoking in their uniforms and talking in solemn voices about a dance act they'd seen on a television talent show the night before. When eventually they saw us, they hurriedly finished their cigarettes and made their way along the path back to the main part of the hospital. 'Ladies,' my father said as they passed, nodding and half rising from his chair as though they had just left the captain's table of a cruise ship.

'I may be dying, but I've still got it,' he said. 'You see the arse on that?' – he pointed to the woman's shuddering rear – 'I should have asked you for that. What a last request that would have been!'

He said he was dying in the same way he would have once have said he was drunk or ugly; not quite believing that he was anything of the kind. There was foam at the corner of his lip which he caught with his hand. That was something my grandfather used to do: let spit dribble from the corner of his mouth and mop it up with a handkerchief. I used to look at my sister and gag at the sight of it; the false teeth that had so amused us as children now foul things that sat crooked in his mouth, leaking liquid down his chin. Dad would mock him, his manners and his appearance. I wondered if he remembered that, and whether he felt bad about it.

Dad looked nothing like Grandad though; not then and not ever. Dad was always thin and reedy: a real boneshaker of a man, but he had become more cadaverous since the illness had taken hold. Under the yellow lights he looked even more unwell, even closer to death, but his rakish smile intimated that he knew something even the doctors didn't. I held the blue Bic lighter I'd purchased from the newsagents in my pocket – he would not use matches, he said they gave him headaches – and thought that when people say they laugh in the face of death they don't mean it literally; my Dad, however, certainly did.

'It's not going to light itself, soft lad,' he said. 'Come on, step to it. Chop, chop.'

I handed him the lighter and he tried to flip the wheel. His hands were shaking, his flesh loose over his bones. These were old man's hands. Had someone said he was seventy, no one would have disagreed: the deterioration was faster even than his diagnosis. I convinced my mother to visit him early in his treatment but when she saw him from a distance she grabbed me by the arm, apologized and turned on her heels. When I called round later, to her and Jim's place, she was sitting on the big leatherette sofa looking at old photographs of him and her, pictures of us as children.

'It doesn't make me hate him any less,' she said as she offered tea but poured gin. 'Don't think that. I've been many things in this life, love, but I've never been a hypocrite and I won't start now. Not for you, and especially not for him.'

We got slowly drunk. I cried and she cried, though she made it clear her tears were for me. 'Do you remember,' she said as we ate a defrosted chilli and drank red wine, 'when you were about seven and you decided that you and Elsie needed a new daddy? You said to me that your other friends had new daddies and you wanted one too. You remember that?'

'I suggested Mr Stevens,' I said. 'He had a snooker table and a sports car.'

'He ended up marrying that Skellern woman. Josie from Jim's work knows her a bit and she got chatting to him. Bald like Yul Brynner he is now, apparently.'

'Does he still have the snooker table?' I said.

She smiled. 'I'll make sure she asks next time.'

Dad never mentioned Mum, and I never told him how close she came to seeing him. He hadn't expected much in the way of visitors, which was fortunate. Elsie hadn't been in contact for over a decade and, like Mum, refused to be a hypocrite. I went to gather his drinking buddies at the North Star. They all promised to come later, on another day, soon though, really soon. Even when I went back to tell them that it wasn't going to be long, that now was the time, they just looked at Lank Tony behind the bar.

'He was a right pain in the arse, your Ray,' Lank Tony said. 'I mean he'd give you his last fag and fivepence, sure, but still a right pain in the arse. Drink for Ray, though, eh? A drink for Ray.' I watched the five of them toast him with whisky and exchange the same glances: *I hope it's you next, I hope it's not me.*

My father knew nothing of this. He'd look through the papers, laughing at celebrities and politicians. *That Amy Winehouse? She looks like one of those blokes I was in Pentonville with once, just with more tattoos and smaller tits.* I'd let him make the jokes and wonder why it was only me here. Just the two of us. Two men with nothing in common, not even sport, not even the fucking football. It was the only time in my life that I was glad of his jokes. At least it kept the conversation flowing.

I watched him flip the wheel on the lighter, again and again. He adjusted the flame setting then tried again. At the fourth time of asking still nothing happened. He took the cigarette from his mouth and held it up, the filter wet with his saliva. 'Would you, son? I think this has got the old man lock on.'

I took the clammy cigarette, lit it and passed it back. He held it between his thumb and forefinger – like a spiv, Mum had always said. He put the cigarette to his lips. The last cigarette. This last, final cigarette. He sucked in the smoke and filled his lungs.

○

Ray sips his coffee and takes a second pull on his cigarette. He is trying not to smoke too quickly, which has been his habit all his life and is probably what's killed him. It seems a very slow kind of suicide, and one that in a race with the bottle always looked on the outside track. He blows out the smoke and a Cadillac drives past, ice-cream coloured and with the top down. In the back is Yul Brynner, at least it looks like Yul Brynner from up there. The guy is bald as an egg and three girls are with him in the back of the Cadillac. But it can't be Yul Brynner because he died four years ago, sixty-five and change, fifteen more than Ray will ever see. Ray watches the car pull away and hears the giggling of the girls. He will never know what it feels like to go bald, to have to shave the hairs at the back of his head to match his crown. He's ambivalent about that part.

Yul Brynner made a commercial to be broadcast after he died, saying that if he'd stopped the smoking then he wouldn't be talking about the cancer. Ray doesn't see it that way. He lets out a long beam of Chesterfield smoke in satisfaction. He couldn't have written without the cigarettes, he's certain of that. The drinking stopped him from writing, but the cigarettes? They sharpened his mind. He knows that the routine of smoking helped him so many times to get out of a rut, out of another story-shaped hole.

With the cigarette smouldering, he coughs again but it isn't a bad one, not this time. He is enjoying the cigarette, it feels light underneath the thumbnail of his right hand. He flicks it just to make sure it is still there. Ash falls on the floor and is kicked up a little on a breeze that passes across the balcony.

The problem is that Ray's enjoying this cigarette so much he's already looking forward to the next one. If he were rich, he imagines that he would like to smoke only a third of each cigarette then immediately light another. If he'd met Tess earlier, if her hot streak had started years before, then maybe he could have done just that. Maybe that would have saved him from this.

You shouldn't get hung up on things, but when you're doing something for the final time it's hard not to. He thinks of Maryann. Sixteen when she gave birth the first time, seventeen the second. He has students now whom he teaches and he can't see any kind of correlation between their fresh eighteen-year-old selves and Maryann and Ray, two babies on their knees, the sawmill dust in his hair, the smell of disinfectant on his skin. And as he thinks about it, he realizes that even when they had no money, even when they were on the verge of bankruptcy there were always cigarettes. They were always there. They were a reliance and they were reliable. No matter how bad the day, you could come home and smoke one and it might just feel that the world wasn't such a terrible place after all.

Ray shakes his head at this. The last book is complete; it is poetry and he is glad to have finished it. He has left everything in order: neat. His last story, 'Errand', is about the death of a writer and though proud of it, he is also worried about how it looks. That it is too poignant. He does not want to be remembered that way. He does not know how he wishes to be remembered. It's not something that anyone should have the chance to consider, he thinks. You should be doing what it is you'll be remembered for, rather than working out what that thing is. Even if it's being a total ass.

○

The smoke my father blew from his mouth was thin, as though it was just the steam coming from his lungs. His hands shook as he held the cigarette and we both watched the Saturday night traffic go by: the buses, the motorbikes, the sports cars with their spoilers. I sat down on a wooden bench and pulled my jumper's sleeves over my hands. It was getting cold.

'I do appreciate it, you know,' he said. 'You doing this.'

'I just wheeled you out here, that's all,' I said.

'And I appreciate it. Giving a dying man his dying wish. Did you . . .' He paused for a moment and shifted himself in the chair. His face was expectant and I would have loved nothing more than to say no. That in the rush of leaving I had forgotten; that it was unfortunate but he would have to go without. Instead I passed him the hip-flask.

'Good lad,' he said. He put the cigarette in the crook of his mouth and squinted as he unscrewed the cap. The coal of the cigarette glowed as he puffed on it; then he took a long pull from the flask.

'Forgot to tell you. Heard a good one this morning.'

It was a long joke about beekeepers and I'd heard it before. In fact I thought it was him who'd told me, one afternoon in the North Star perhaps. I sat back down on the bench and tried to fix him in my mind: the last cigarette, probably the last time I would ever be alone with him. He took a gummy pull on the fag and then raised his arm at the punchline. I laughed and it sounded hollow in the night air. He drank some more Scotch and nodded his head.

'You remember when we went fishing that time?' I said. 'You remember that?'

He paused and hitched up his robe a little.

'Aye, right. It were just the two of us. It pissed it down and you cried because it was cold. And to cheer you up I ate some of the bait' – he slapped his thighs and laughed – 'I can see you now, your little rod barely in the water and you screaming to go back home.'

'It wasn't just the two of us, though, was it?' I said. 'Lank Tony was there. And Stan. You only let me go because Mum had to go to work and she couldn't get someone to watch me.'

He looked confused. 'If you say so,' he said. 'I thought it was just us two. Don't remember Tony or Stan there at all.' He shook his head and took a long drag. He looked away from me, over to the road and the silent terraced houses opposite. 'Fact is I don't remember much about all that time, you know? Seems so long ago now. Another life.'

'I remember once you bought me an ice cream,' I said. 'As a surprise.'

'Ah yes, I do remember that,' he said, as though it was important. 'Beautiful day. Sweating like a wog on a rape charge, I was. Bought you all an ice cream. Your mum was right surprised, I can tell you. I'd remembered that she liked those ice creams with the bubble gum in the bottom, you see. She thought it was romantic.'

'No,' I said. 'No, another time. When we were on Alton Way.'

It must have been a year or so before he left. Mum had taken Elsie into town to buy something she needed. Dad and I were alone and watching the television. Outside an ice-cream van sounded its three-blind-mice tune and I went to the window and watched it slowly make its way down the road. It wasn't too hot a day, but it was hot enough. Dad picked up the paper and said he was going for a dump. I turned away from the window and watched the television. When I heard the door open, I looked round thinking it might be Mum and Elsie, but it was him clutching a

99 Flake with strawberry sauce in each hand. 'He asked if I wanted a ninety-nine,' he said. 'And I said I wanted a bloody hundred.'

I retold the story and he looked on with growing confusion.

'If you say so, son. Can't say I remember though.' He sucked in some more smoke. 'And, anyway, I don't even like strawberry sauce.'

He laughed and beckoned me to pass the flask. I hoped he wasn't going to get pissed. How would that look, my dying father drunk, stinking of fags and booze, trying to goose the nurses during the early morning rounds? He took a long pull and passed back the flask. I looked at the floor and at the wheels of the chair. There was mud in the tread and the red paint was chipped.

'I miss fishing,' he said eventually.

○

Ray looks at the chunky wedding ring and thinks of the kids. He has variably been a good father, a bad father, an absent father, and a recovering father. Being a father is a lot of people to be; and he's glad that at the final reckoning both his daughter and his son realize that he is more the good father, the recovering father than anything else. Like being a smoker, being a father becomes him, and he feels that truly as he takes another drag on the Chesterfield. Like the smoking, there would be no writing without the kids; their scratched knees, their bathing routines and their bedtimes. They are adults now, but that means nothing when your father dies. Everyone's a child then.

He places the cigarette on the edge of the table and moves inside again, twisting the cord of the telephone under the doors. He has never made a phone call from a hotel room before, the cost so prohibitive he's never even considered it. Usually he would use one of the booths in the lobby, but there is money on the dresser and this is a call he doesn't mind paying for.

Ray punches in the digits, pausing on the middle one and remembering with sudden clarity that it is a number 8. There is a brief pause before the call is connected. It rings twice and a female voice answers.

'Hi, Diane, it's Ray,' he says.

'Oh, hi, Ray,' Diane says, smiling. 'How was it all? You both have yourselves a good time?'

'It was great, Diane. We got hitched at one of those little chapels and then we had steaks and went gambling. Tess is up about six hundred bucks.'

'And you're feeling okay?' Diane ties the telephone cord around her little finger.

'Never better, Diane.' He picks up the cigarette and takes another hit.

'Still smoking though. I can hear it.'

'It's my last one ever. Promise. It's a Chesterfield.'

'And how is it?' she says. She quit two years before and often feels like starting again when she's around Ray.

'Like heaven,' he says and laughs. 'Is he in? Can you put him on? I want to speak with him.'

'Sure, Ray, I'll go get him.' She puts her hands over the receiver. 'Honey!' she shouts. 'Quickly, it's your dad on the phone.'

○

A woman was approaching, striding stiff-legged and purposefully up the asphalt pathway. She had a duffel coat on over her uniform and her displeasure was obvious from the way she pumped her arms. It was Diane.

'Looks like we've been rumbled,' I said. 'Diane's here. Throw the cigarette away.'

'I will do no such thing,' Dad said. 'Fuck her, I'm smoking a fag.'

He smiled revealing his teeth and the gap by his left molar. They say beards grow when you die, toenails too. Dad was always doing things of his own accord.

'Please,' I said, but it was too late.

'Mr Peters. Are you smoking a cigarette?' Diane said.

'No, it's a hamster,' he said.

She rolled her eyes at me and looked down at Dad.

'And you've been drinking, haven't you?'

'Only deep from the well of life, my glorious Florence Nightingale.'

'It is against hospital policy for patients—'

'Oh do shut up, woman. Let me finish this wee fag and then I'll be in. Scout's honour.'

She looked at me in exasperation and I shrugged. She motioned towards me and I followed her a little way off.

'You let him smoke any more and it could kill him right now,' Diane said. 'I'm serious. He's got a chance. It's slim, but there's a chance, okay?'

'He asked me to. And I—'

'I know, Lindsay,' she said. 'I know. Just make sure it's his last one, okay?'

We looked over at him in the chair, his low voice humming 'Smoke On the Water'. Diane squeezed my arm.

'And you're okay? Coping?'

'Coping. Yes.'

'Good.'

She nodded and headed back to the ward. I sat back down on the bench.

'If I were you, son,' he said. 'I'd try and get in her knickers. Everyone knows nurses are filthy as fuck.'

○

'Hey, Dad,' Lindsay says. He is dressed in pyjamas. It is late morning and the smell of pancakes has made it to the top of the stairs. He sits on the side of the bed and rubs his eyes. Since they found out he has hardly slept, hardly done anything but think of his father, his father who's not going to be around for ever. Not even for a few more years.

Diane tells him to be positive, but he can't find the positives in any of this.

'Hey, son. How you doing?'

'Not good, Dad. How about you?'

'Better, son. Tess has won maybe six hundred bucks gambling. Looks like I'm going to die rich after all.'

Ray takes a drag on his almost finished cigarette.

'It's early morning in Reno. It's beautiful here.'

'Reno's a shit hole, Dad.'

'I know, Lin. I know' — he blows out smoke — 'but for the moment it's the best place on earth. I was thinking that the only thing that'd make it better was if you were all waiting downstairs in the buffet room. All of you waiting and then me and Tess could come down and have breakfast with you all. Wouldn't that be something?'

'I'd like that, Dad. I'd like that a lot,' Lindsay says.

'You're going to come and see me, right?' There is a long pause. Lindsay's crying but he won't let his father know. Ray is crying too.

'Either next week or week after. Depends on shifts,' he says. On the bedside dresser there is an old black and white photo of his mum and dad on their wedding day, a picture of his mother, and another picture of his father. It's hard to look at him and hear him speak.

'Make it sooner rather than later,' Ray says, sucking in some smoke and letting it drift out of his mouth. 'I don't want to go without having seen you properly.' There is a pause.

'Listen, son, I know I wasn't always—'

'Hey, Dad,' he says, 'not now. There's no need for that now.'

'I love you, son,' he says and now the tears are coming down his face. He can taste them on his lips. They taste right in his tobacco-heavy mouth. 'I've not said it enough in my life but I'm proud of you and I love you.'

Ray takes the last draw from his final cigarette, then flicks it away; the last of the smoke coming out from his nose: the last of the smoke from the final cigarette.

'You too, Dad,' Lindsay says. 'You too.'

○

Sitting on the bench, I watched Diane return through the double doors. We were going out together the following week; up to the William IV and then on perhaps to the Greek restaurant up on the Lea Bridge Road. That Thursday she was moving from Oncology over to Obs and Gynae, which meant she didn't feel like she was breaking any rules.

'You're going to come and see me, right?' Dad said. There was a long pause and then I nodded. He looked at the cigarette and blew a beam of smoke over its end.

I thought about Diane, wondering whether she would be less hesitant when Dad was finally dead. I kicked at the ground, wishing I could dislodge thoughts like that as easily.

'Make it sooner rather than later,' Dad said, sucking in smoke and letting it drift out of his mouth. 'I reckon you could get away with wheeling me out here again. I mean, I feel fine, so what fucking harm is one more smoke going to cause, eh? What do these fucking doctors know, anyway? They can't even write properly! You should see the sheets, looks like fucking Urdu or something. Probably is Urdu. Probably the official language of the NHS these days. What do you call a Paki doctor and a Jewish nurse—'

'Hey, Dad,' I said. 'Not now. There's no need for that now. No need at all.'

'You know, son,' he said with a crooked toothed smile. 'I know you've looked after me and all that, but sometimes you can be a right arsehole, you know that? A right pain in the arse.'

He took the last draw from his final cigarette, then flicked it away; the last of the smoke coming out of his nose: the last of the smoke from what might have been his final cigarette.

'You too, Dad,' I said. 'You too.'

# Acknowledgements

I am grateful for the support of a number of people in the writing of this collection.

Andrew Kidd, for cutting both fish and foxes; and believing when I didn't.

Kate Harvey, for making these stories better than I ever could have hoped; Martin Bryant for the copy edit, and everyone at Picador and Pan Macmillan.

For inspiration, help and advice: Kirstie Addis, Lisa Baker, Nicholson Baker, Christine Bolland, Sarah Castleton, Emma Conally, Andrew Gallix, Niven Govinden, Aidan Jackson, Peter Lavery, Paula McGoverny, David Mitchell, Chris Paling, Gavin Pilgrim, Lee Rourke, Jeremy Trevathan, Tim Thornton, Jeannette Walker.

Aravind Adiga, Wells Tower, David Vann and Evie Wyld for their support and kind words.

Salena Godden, Rachel Rayner and everyone at the Book Club Boutique.

Fans of Gary Alexander. Former residents of Hartington Road. Thanks to you all.

## *Acknowledgements*

Rebecca Bream, David Stewart, Samuel Stewart; Daniel Fordham and Jude Rogers; Hyun Sook Shin, Juno Shepherd: my London family.

William Atkins for his wisdom and understanding; Guy Griffiths for being a genius; Nikesh Shukla for being a superhero.

Oliver Shepherd – best friend, first reader, rock.

Gareth Evers – brother, teacher, bête noir.

My parents, Joyce and John Evers, for their love and support, no matter what.

Tracy Murray – for everything.

The stories in this collection are dedicated to Barry Abraham. I hope he'd have found them mildly interesting.

# picador.com

blog
videos
interviews
extracts